Justify The Means

Claudia –
You rock!,
Please let me know
what you think of the book!
Madison McGraw

Justify The Means

Madison McGraw

iUniverse, Inc.
New York Lincoln Shanghai

Justify The Means

iUniverse, Inc.

For information address:
iUniverse, Inc.
2021 Pine Lake Road, Suite 100
Lincoln, NE 68512
www.iuniverse.com

ISBN: 0-595-28812-X

Printed in the United States of America

This is for my mother, Fran. We could be sure to find her snuggled in her ratty red robe, reading her way through piles of books when she wasn't screaming at the TV because the Miami Dolphins were losing…again.

And for my father, Bob. His life on this earth too short, yet long enough to touch so many lives. He never failed me as a father and as he was dying, he somehow managed to become not only my best friend, but a hero.

To Sara, Josh, and Katie, the 'stars' of my life.

To Al…the most dedicated cop and dad that I know.

Darin (and Adam) for always bailing me out.

Gary for the journey and making this possible.

Special thanks to Detective Ray Kuter of the Montgomery County (Pa) District Attorney's Office.

Finally, this book is for all the families that have been shattered by victimization at the hands of pedophiles. My greatest hope is that peace can be found among the pain.

Please be sure to visit my website…www.chicksdigbooks.com
Or email me @ chicksdigbooks@comcast.net

Injustice is relatively easy to bear; it is justice that hurts.

—*H.L. Mencken*

The front door is painted blue. Midnight blue; the color of an eggplant, the color of a bruise that never seems to heal. The doorbell glows as I press a gloved finger on it. Ding Dong.

My heart is beating as if I've consumed five cups of coffee loaded with sugar. In my right hand, I hold a small package wrapped in brown paper and in the other hand, a clipboard, but tucked in my waistband is the real reason I'm here.

The sun, high in the sky, press hot rays on the top of my head like an angry hand.

The door swings open and there he stands. Loser. Or should I say, GONER.

"T-Ray Austin?" My voice is friendly, like I'm as sweet as fresh spun cotton candy.

He is tall. His skin is white and slightly clumpy around the cheeks; like paste I used in elementary school. His hair is powdery and in need of a trim. Smells of dirty socks and cigarette smoke escape from the house. Bile rises in my throat. I swallow hard.

"Yes?" He eyes the package.

"This is for you." I hand him the empty box, then the clipboard, taking care not to come into contact with his hands. The sight of his bony fingers makes the hairs on the back of my neck bristle. Those hands are evil. I know where they have been and what they have done. There is no hesitation as my hand lifts the gun and I point it at his forehead.

His gray eyes look at the weapon, then shift back to my eyes, and then I pull the trigger.

He falls back, hitting the door.

Just as I imagined it would be.

I grab the box and the clipboard.

Rule 1: Never leave anything behind.

"Fucking sick Bastard," I mutter as I walk calmly to the van parked at the curb.

I wondered how this would feel, taking someone's life. I'm surprised to find that I feel a bit lighter, relieved. As if I've walked out of church after giving confession.

I'm hungry. Starved. Planning a murder isn't conducive to eating. I haven't had much of an appetite. I've been eating light for two weeks; a salad, a half a sandwich, a bag of chips. Now I feel like wolfing down a steak, a baked potato slathered in butter and sour cream. To top it off, a dessert of strawberry shortcake bursting with juicy, plump, berries.

I slide into the driver's seat, put on my seatbelt and catch my reflection in the rear view mirror. For the first time in weeks there is a genuine smile.

Detective Bennigan
August 2, Friday

I'm stretched out on a lounge chair. The scent of coconut suntan lotion fills the air. I'm praying that the population of North Twilight keeps their knives, guns, and anger under control until I can have a full day of rest. The bikini I'm wearing is snug around the hips. I swear to Badge, my year old chocolate lab who is panting under the lounge chair, that I will throw away all the Cheetos, oatmeal cream pies, and frozen mozzarella sticks first thing…tomorrow.

"C'mon, Badge," I reason with the only one around to listen to me, "ya gotta have that day before the diet to eat yourself into such a frenzy that your stomach reminds you for days after that you really shouldn't have consumed the whole snack food aisle of the 7-11."

The sun is climbing to its perch; it's as hot and unforgiving as a Latin Lover done wrong. Beads of sweat mix with the suntan oil; my skin feels as greasy as extra buttered movie theater popcorn. I stretch my long arms (my brother got the long legs; I got arms that look best in sleeveless shirts) above my head and let out a sigh of contentment.

A whole day off. Zoey safely tucked away at daycare. After turning 3 last week she was moved into the preschool room. She thinks it's cool to have a coloring box that belongs only to her, that naptime was reduced by half an hour. She doesn't cry when I drop her off anymore, cutting my guilt in half.

Ben, my ex-husband, is picking Zoey up after school. Father and daughter will spend the whole weekend together, leaving me with time, time, nothing but time. I feel giddy, thinking of all the things I can do to fill my empty weekend. Clean (ha ha ha). I could see a movie that doesn't involve animated animals. I could drive the 30 minutes to Philadelphia and take advantage of living close to a historical city. But why leave North Twilight? We have; a 3 story mall, 3 major bookstores, 7 mega theater complexes, a small zoo, too many bars to count (most have the word 'pub' somewhere in the title). Our restaurants are as various as the fine citizens of our community; Japanese, Mexican, Italian, Greek, Chinese, American Bistro, Southern, Western, and two places so fancy the waiters stand at your table and wait for you to put your fork down so they can give you a clean one. Frankly, I prefer the hoagie shops where the guys behind the counter call everyone 'hun' or 'buddy' and give me extra mayo cause I'm cute (long arms and all).

I turn onto my stomach, reach under the chair to rub Badge's ears.

"Hey Badge, maybe if you're lucky I'll take you to Becky's house tomorrow and she'll let you swim in the pool." He thumps his tail, and his toffee eyes beg, "Please, please, please."

"And maybe if I'm lucky, I'll get lucky tonight."

A breeze scoots the clouds across the sky. My pony tailed auburn hair sways back and forth tickling my shoulders. I'd been a blonde for a few months. I'm as fickle about my hair color as I am my men. Being blonde has its advantages. More cat whistles. More turned heads. But finding respect is like OJ Simpson finding the person who really killed his wife. Before having my golden head, I would flash my badge, announce "Homicide" and elicit awe and fear. I changed my hair back to auburn when, after declaring myself a detective, the perp gave me a toothless smile and looked me up and down, undressing me with his eyes then laughing, "I'm on Candid Camera, right? Will I get paid for this?"

My cell phone rings and without thinking, I flip it open, expecting it to be Becky. Becky's been my best friend since the third grade when she taught me how to make fake fingernails using glue and a ruler.

"Hey." I sing into the phone.

"Hey yourself," a low, hollow, voice slithers over the phone. It's definitely not Becky.

A frown robs my smile. "Tom…you're calling to tell me that I forgot to hand in some paperwork?"

Please let it be paperwork, please, please, please. I sit up and look to the sky. I swear to God that if this is not a serious call, that if it doesn't ruin my weekend, I will go to church on Sunday. I won't take communion though because it's been like, 16 years since my last confession (Catholic school Graduation Mass), and I'd be struck down.

Badge rakes his paws across the grass and pulls himself out from under the chair. He sniffs my toes, his dry tongue slips out and he starts to lick my foot.

"Stop, stop, that's sick!" I squeal, leaping up from the chair so fast it flips onto its side.

"Uh, I take it you're not alone?" Tom clears his throat.

"I'm alone, I'm alone." I sigh; I've been alone every night since Ben left seven months ago.

Okay. I lied.

There was that night in June. With the dentist. But it doesn't count. Had I known what he did for a living, there never would have been a sleep over (I should have realized something was wrong when he got up to brush his teeth before, during and after sex). I have an aversion to men who like to stick needles and pokey instruments into mouths. Not to mention…what kind of person could actually YANK and PULL and TWIST a tooth out of soft, pillowy, gums?

Tom clears his throat again. "Have you been drinking Maggie? Because if so…"

"Oh Jesus, Tom. No, I have not been drinking. My dog was licking my toes. They have suntan lotion on them." I shove my feet into yellow flip-flops.

"My cat licks my hair when I'm sleeping. Sometimes, I'll wake up and there he is, licking my hair with his scratchy tongue."

"That's gross, Tom."

"Actually, it kinda feels good except he's got really bad breath. Smells like seven day old tuna."

"Okay, you know what Tom…that sounds like a personal problem. Now, why did you call?" I cross my fingers and slide the back door open, easing myself into the house. I'd spent the last three weeks working on a murder case that my partner and I had solved quickly; it was just a matter of making sure we dotted all i's and crossed all t's so the case held up in court.

"Your paperwork is fine as far as I know. I'm calling because you need to respond to 328 Burnt Hill Road. There's been a murder. Jake is already on his way."

I stand in the middle of the kitchen (okay, war zone). Bowls and plates fill the sink. Dried bits of oatmeal, egg, and spaghetti sauce hug the dishes. The stovetop is crusted with particles of food that will take a metal scraper and some bicep work to loosen. The other rooms are just as bad.

One of the things I miss about Ben is his passion for cleaning. Wouldn't watch a sports event without making sure the living room was clean. And he never complained about the aversion I had to sponges, mops, and dust cloths. Ben never yelled at me for leaving the newspaper on the floor, the butter on the counter, the top off the toothpaste. But his remarkable cleaning skills didn't make up for his snoring. Nor the fact that the only thing he was mechanically inclined for was replacing the batteries in the remote control. I changed the oil in my car *and* his car. I hooked up the new dryer. I put a CD burner on the computer. He dusted. I put shelves in the garage. I fixed broken screens. He vacuumed.

"328 Burnt Hill Road?" I scrawl the address on the back of an unopened water bill.

"Yep."

"That sounds familiar." I flip-flop my way upstairs, stepping over a baby doll, a coloring book.

328 Burnt Hill Road…

"Oh God, that's T-Ray Austin's house, right?" I ask.

"The one and only."

I sit down on the top step, leaning against the railing. Badge lay beside me, pressing his wet nose against my thigh.

"Is he dead?"

"I reckon so."

"I'll be there in fifteen minutes." I snap the phone shut and smile. A dirty house and a deeper tan didn't really matter now. This murderous event was worth the premature end of my leisure time.

As I dig through the closet for something clean, I dial Becky.

"Hey, you're interrupting my Court TV," she yammers after answering on the second ring. "I think the Judge is going to rule on the sequester issue. You should see David Westerfield; his face is all twitchy like he's got some sort of seizure condition."

Becky is addicted to Court TV. It started with the Danielle van Dam case. A little girl kidnapped from her bed. She was found a month later; her body dumped in a field, ravaged by animals, by the weather. Just as shocking, was that the van Dam's neighbor, David Westerfield, was the man charged with the crime. Becky called everyday with updates on the trial. Sometimes I worried if the jury didn't find David Westerfield guilty of the murder of little Danielle, she'd hop a plane to California and seek her own justice. Though she could barely squash a spider without gagging.

"Sorry, Beck. But I have good news and bad news."

"We're still going out tonight, right? Marty is taking Susie to cheerleading practice. I'm kid free. Husband free. I planned on drinking my limit of three margaritas. I haven't been to the Tex Mex since you threw that little congrats party for Jake and Lucy on the announcement of her pregnancy."

"That was nine months ago!" I find a pair of not so wrinkled tan, cotton, pants under some towels that may or may not be dirty. I have one blue polo shirt hanging in the closet with the inscription "North Twilight Police Department" embroidered in white stitching above the left breast. I don't have time for a shower. I pull the clothes over my bikini; they cling to my skin like Saran Wrap clings to hot buttered corn on the cob. I hate to be last on the scene. It's like walking into a party after introductions have been made and everyone is shit-faced.

"I know it was nine months ago. That's why I HAVE to go tonight." Becky whines. She is Queen of the Whine, but the best wife, mother, and friend, I've ever known, so I forgive the whining, the Court TV, the fact she has the build of a ballerina yet eats Twinkies, Zingers, Fritos, and hot dogs with all the fixings. I also forgive her for calling me in the middle of the night when Marty is working at the firehouse because she thinks there is a ghost hovering in the hall closet and 'could I come over with my gun to check it out?' It's the only time she'll allow a gun in her house. She doesn't understand that if there was a ghost, a weapon would be pointless. I've tried to explain…but it makes her feel better, so I just drag myself over.

Becky is also my conscious. She's the person who keeps me in line, keeps my head on straight. Sometimes I'm attracted to the other side of the road; where shadows filled with temptation lurk behind hazy street lamps. I could easily imagine myself hopping from bar to bar a few nights a week if I were single and childless. I've been tempted by every vice known to man and walked away. I wish I could say I'm proud that I'm able to say "Thanks, but no thanks" when it comes to drugs that make things happy and good and relaxing…or having sex for the pure pleasure of it and then moving on to the next romp…but the truth is, a little part of me wishes I would give in.

Part of the reason I became a cop was to keep me on the right side of the street. I'm able to stand on the curb and view the wilder side without getting run over. First row seats to the best live theater show there ever was.

"There's been a murder." I push my feet into sandals. "I can't say for sure until I get to the scene, BUT, I'm almost 100% sure it's someone you despise."

"That guy who owns the 7-11 and always tries to charge me extra if I use two creamers for my coffee?"

"No." I laugh, "Guess again. Think local news story."

"Hmmm…"

"Jeezz…" I bounce down the stairs, grabbing my duffle bag and purse. "Think pervert."

"Oh...My...God...T-Ray Austin?"

"Sounds like it. Don't go telling anyone, not even Marty. Tom called with the news and you know Tom..."

"Oh yeah, Tom the dispatcher. I thought you guys canned him after he told a woman she was a fucking retard because she called the station to report a bat in her attic."

"No, they kept him because he said he thought it was Nate playing a prank."

"I could see Nate doing something like that."

"So could the Chief. Anyway, would you be able to drop by and take care of Badge for me? He's been cooped up almost all week, and no telling when I'll get home to let him out again."

"Sure, not a problem. I'll bring him over here. He can go swimming."

"Thanks so much. God, you are such a great friend." I bend down and kiss the top of Badge's head. He gives me a warm lick.

"I swear I'll do my best to meet you at the Tex Mex. I've got to find someone other than a dog to kiss me."

"Well, you could still have Ben...and there's always Mr. Clean Teeth."

"Stop it." I slide into my Mustang. A lollipop left on the dashboard has melted into a gooey, purple, mess.

"And disregard the condition of my house; I think a cyclone sped through it when I was sleeping."

"You know what they say...when all is right with the home, all is right with the love and life."

"In that case," I throw the car into reverse, "I'm doomed forever."

> "I must do something" always solves more problems than "Something must be done."
>
> —Author Unknown

I wouldn't say I snapped. I didn't wake up one day, fry some eggs, brew some coffee and decide to kill T-Ray Austin. I'd been following the story from the beginning. How could I avoid it? It was in the papers daily. It started ten months ago with his arrest for 'allegedly' molesting three boys on a baseball team he coached. Shortly after, readers were surprised to learn he had moved to North Twilight from Florida where he had done time for the same exact thing, five years ago.

The police found a ton of child pornography on his computer. The trial started in July; it should have been an easy conviction. Then a fastball was thrown in the courtroom; no one had a mitt, and it struck the prosecution center mass.

T-Ray's mother called several of the jurors and begged them to find her son innocent. Judge Wallace declared a mistrial, and because the prison was full, remanded T-Ray Austin to his home, under electronic surveillance until the start of the new trial.

This all came about at a time when heinous crimes against children were at an all time high; Danielle van Dam, Samantha Runnion, Elizabeth Smart, Ashley Pond, Miranda Gaddis. These are the children we know about, brought to us by urgent, sorrowful newscasters. There are many other missing children that, for one reason or another, never caught the attention of the media.

The abduction stories that made it past the teleprompter were soon cast aside because life goes on; there are more important things to worry about like the decline and rally of the stock market, the misuse of funds by management of Fortune 500 *companies. Could Martha Stewart, Queen of cake and all things made with a glue gun, be a corporate trader? Who will The Bachelor give the last rose to? And was Winona Ryder researching a movie role when security cameras captured her smuggling clothes out of Bloomingdale's?*

I was sick to death. Sick of reading that these pedophiles were getting two to five years for defiling a child. Sick of the ACLU crying that it wasn't fair for a child molester (who had been convicted and done his time) to report his whereabouts to the police when he was paroled, to make his past known to the community. The bleeding hearts cried: "The guy has done his time, he deserves a fresh start!" I call these morons accomplices. They are the people who stand by these creeps, idiots demanding that pedophiles receive a second, third, and fourth chance.

Rarely did anyone demand, "What about the child? Where is his fresh start? Who will give his innocence back?"

Oh, I'm not naïve. Not in the least bit. I know there is madness in the world. There is sickness. Minds so full of sleaze no amount of whitewashing will erase the perversion that clings to their brain matter like a starving tick feeding on a fat dog.

Why do these crimes against children keep happening? Because to get anything done in this fine American system, to make drastic changes, there is a ton of paperwork, proper channels to swim and political sharks circling the water. I understand that, I understand it well. But I don't agree with it. Not anymore. Not when the children of this country are suffering great tragedies. Families are being ripped into shreds.

Imagine the mother and father of an abducted child closing their eyes at night to find sleep but instead of darkness, they are flooded with images of their child being violated, strangled, and left naked for the world to see.

They couldn't protect them.

The police couldn't protect them.

The lawmakers couldn't protect them. The lawmakers couldn't protect them.

The lawmakers couldn't protect them.

If there is a God, he couldn't protect them.

In my mind it is clear. Anyone who harms a child in any sexual manner deserves nothing better than to be thrown into a hole in the ground, still breathing. Those lives scarred by him will be invited to the gravesite. They can release their anger, their sadness and their pain by shoveling dirt until the hole is filled. Cement will then seal the grave; seal a part of their suffering.

It wasn't that I snapped one day. It was the gradual hollowness that was carved into my soul each time I heard of a new abduction, a new molestation. When the idea to kill T-Ray Austin came to me, it wasn't in a dream. No one spoke to me from beyond. It was just something that had to be done. As simple as scratching an itch. It is done because of a need, and it provides much relief.

I only planned on one murder; a sort of hat tip to the children who had lost their lives this year and to the boys whose innocence had been stolen by T-Ray.

No one would ever suspect me. I am the person you pass on the street and smile at. I am someone that you would ask to stay at your house while you are away. I'm your best friend. I'm the family favorite.

I had no doubts I could right some wrongs.

I could no longer be a bystander to the tragedy. The suffering. The virtuousness lost. What I was doing was against the law as the law is written. But really, what I was doing was right when it came to laws of the heart. Sometimes, the end justifies the means.

Detective Bennigan
August 2, Friday. Afternoon

"Looks like a .38 service revolver." Jake and I squat next to the body lying face up on the hardwood floor. A puddle of crimson blood has escaped from the dead man's head; I'm careful not to get anywhere near the thick liquid.

"Maybe a 9mm?" I ask.

"Could be," Jake sniffs the air as he stands up, holding out his arm to make sure I don't accidentally step in the body fluids. "You smell like a Pina Colada."

"I was sun tanning." I smooth the wrinkles from my shirt and take a deep breath, trying to smell my own skin.

"You should have kept your swimsuit on." Lee chimes in as he snaps pictures of the body. He is the oldest of the detectives. One year shy of retirement, one minute away from a heart attack; his body plump and pink like a summer tomato.

"I have it on underneath my clothes," I wink.

"Maggie," Jake frowns.

I raise my eyebrows in question.

"This is a crime scene," Jake whispers, glancing around the room. Four uniformed cops are performing various duties. Jake nods towards a kid who looks fresh out of a high school police academy; his face is pale and his eyes are wide with wonder. "We got a rookie among us."

I roll my eyes. Jake is annoyingly honest and adheres to the rules like fresh tar adheres to sneakers. If he is a nickel short at the grocery store and the cashier tells him not to worry about it, he'll run out to his car and search under the seats for change. He never walks across the lawn, choosing the sidewalk even if it means the long way around. If two sodas came out of a vending machine and he only put in enough money for one, he would find a manager and give the extra soda back.

Since the day his wife announced her pregnancy, Jake has been more uptight than usual, causing me to secretly take up my smoking habit. As soon as I'm in my Mustang after a long day with Mr. Underwear Too Tight, I'll light up as soon as I disappear round the bend. Nothing is as relaxing as that first long draw.

As anal as Jake can be, there wasn't one cop who didn't respect him. When it came down to it, every Shield would choose Jake to back them up.

"Jake," I nudge him playfully. "I know you're worried about the birth of your first baby, but relax a little. How is Lucy by the way?"

"She can't sleep. She stays up all night watching reruns of A Baby Story on The Learning Channel. She wakes me up just as the mother is about to give birth and yells, 'See what you did? This is what's going to happen to me.'"

"It's just nerves, Jake." I reassure him.

"I know. I'm just so tired. I've been cleaning, cooking, working. Rubbing her feet every time she gets teary, which is every ten minutes."

Jake did look tired; craggy lines were etched under his usually bright, honey, brown eyes. He wasn't himself. In mind. Or body. For the past three years we've been partners, Jake's skin turned the color of roasted turkey in the summer. He'd spend all his free time on his fishing boat. This summer, however, Jake is as pale as an overcooked noodle. Though I'd never mention it to him (unless he really pissed me off and I wanted to return the favor) I've noticed his body softening, and he's starting to develop a little roll under his waist. Perhaps in sympathy to Lucy's pregnancy. Still, Jake turns heads. He's the typical Italian Stallion with the added bonus of dimpled chin. I think what women find most alluring about him is his devotion to Lucy; a southern belle who is as sweet and refreshing as the silky twang of her voice.

"You want to go interview the guy who found the body?" Jake rocks back on his heels.

It doesn't matter if I say no; I'll have to do it anyway. Jake swears I'm the best at talking to people, he swears I have a sixth sense and can pick up on subtle clues that most other detectives miss, including him.

"I think you'll like him; he's your type." Finally, a smile from Jake. I want to reach out and hold those corners up. The weight of impending fatherhood has kept his sense of humor under a sea of worry…the unspoken fear of what it takes to be a good father. How a baby will affect his job, his winter hockey league, and his relationship with Lucy.

I feel my face soften, "Where is he?"

Leaning against the side of one of the squad cars is Todd Browning. Wearing blue nylon running shorts; Todd's broad chest is bare with the exception of a tuft of curly hair in the concave between his pecs. Short blond hair, matted with sweat, and eyes the color of jealousy.

"I'm Detective Bennigan." I hold out my hand. Though my house looks like a war zone, I find time to squeeze in a manicure. The color of the week is Cherry Pie. A girl has to have priorities.

"Todd Browning." His handshake is firm, but his voice shimmies and twirls in the air like a jazz dancer on speed.

I wince. The body of a God. The mannerisms of a Cosmo covergirl. I'm going to kill Jake.

"So, what happened?" I poise a pen over a new compact notebook.

"I was out running. This is the first time I've ever ran down this street; I usually run on Flagship Road. Then today, I happened to glance up and saw that the name of the street was Burnt Hill Road. That intrigued me." Todd's hands flutter through the air as he speaks, up, down, round, round. As if his wrist joints were greased, as if he were conducting a symphony.

My pen is motionless. I despise the beginning of interviews. No one can stick to the facts. There are usually two pages of bullshit that precede the actual details of what I need to know.

I imagine he drives a white Jetta with a rainbow sticker on the bumper.

"I live over on Candlestick Court. You know that development?"

"I do."

"It's a nice place, great landscaping, but almost every townhouse is filled with your average 3.5 family. Mom, Dad, kid, and dog." He rolls his eyes and sighs.

"So, you were running down Burnt Hill Road…about what time?"

"Hmmm. I guess it must have been half an hour ago. I leave right after the Price Is Right, which means I left at twelve-thirty. What time is it now?"

"One-forty."

"Yeah, that'd be about right, it probably took me about half an hour to run from Candlestick to here. Anyway, I'm running on the sidewalk, looking at the houses, all of which have well kept lawns and shrubs. Then I notice this house." He glances up. "It sticks out like the devil in a Baptist church. Overgrown grass filled with weeds. Cracked porch steps." He shudders.

"Are you a landscaper?" I feel the swell of my toes as I stand two inches away from him, the heat shaking me down like a pissed off mob boss.

"Oh, no Honey, that's just a hobby. I'm a Chippendale dancer. I could get you some free tickets to our show. Some of the guys would love you." He looks me up and down then lets out a long whistle of approval. I'm not sure if it's a good sign that a guy who would probably steal my Victoria Secret lace thongs, eyeliner, and lip gloss, finds me attractive, but who am I to judge?

"We're not all gay, you know." He tells me.

A cloud tucks the sun in its pocket. My shoulders relax in the momentary shade.

"You should try putting some blonde streaks in your hair, around your face to show off your eyes; they are gorgeous."

Unconsciously, my hand flies up to my head. I'd pulled the ponytail out on the drive over.

"Who cuts your hair?" He slides a strand between his fingers.

"Peter cuts my hair, Rebecca does my color. They work for Rapunzel's over on Broad Street in Lansdale, why?"

"They do a great job. You're very stylin for a detective. I love the upward flip. That's very chic right now. Not every woman can wear it, you know."

I'm dying to tell him about my experience as a blonde but Jake is hovering on the front porch. I stick to the subject at hand.

A black Caprice pulls up; Steven Evans, District Attorney is behind the wheel.

"Okay, so you noticed this house; what happened next?"

Todd places his hands on his hips. "Well, the front door was open, and I could see a pair of shoes sticking out. And right away, I think, 'Oh My God, someone had a heart attack!' So I run up the walk and up the steps and then as soon as I get to the top, I see it's a man, and I see the blood. At first, I think he hit his head when he fell. And I'm yelling, "Are you okay? Are you okay?" I step in and I'm about ready to shake him, but when I lean over, I see the hole in his fore-head and I realize he's been shot, and I'm like 'Oh My God, This is so CSI!' Then I figure someone had to put that hole in his head, and I don't know if that someone is still around. I run as fast as I can to the house next door. No one is home. The next house, no one home. Finally, at the house all the way at the end of the block, a little old lady is in the back yard hanging her wash. She lets me use her phone, and I call the police. I came back when the first cop got here. Lee? He should think about shaving his moustache, his top lip is just too thin to support such a crazy amount of hair. At least he should trim it."

I suppress a laugh, give a short wave to the D.A., and think that Todd is probably one of the best witnesses I've ever had, based on entertainment factor.

"Did you touch anything in the house? Did you touch the body?"

Todd shudders. "No, thank God."

"What about the neighborhood? Did you notice any cars, any people?"

"Nope. This place is dead." He bites his lip. "I didn't mean it that way."

"I just need the rest of your information and we'll be in touch. Do you want someone to give you a ride home?"

Todd scratches his head. "I don't know. I think I might need to walk; I've got all this nervous energy now. I've never seen a real dead body before; it's creepy."

I shake his hand and send him on his way. What a waste of a hard body.

Back on the porch, I give Jake and the D.A. the lowdown on my conversation with Todd, hand gestures and all.

"I thought I'd go talk to the little lady down the street. Maybe she saw something."

"Give me a few more minutes here, and I'll go with you." Jake pushes a bead of sweat away from his upper lip.

Most of the uniform patrols have gone, leaving two guys behind. They're sitting in an air-conditioned squad waiting for the next thing we might need help with. Lee has abandoned his camera for the camcorder. And there, in the narrow hallway leading to the back of the house is Nate Hightower. He is dusting the telephone for fingerprints; a lit cigarette is dangling on his bottom lip. It takes two long strides before I'm standing at his side.

"Jesus, Nate!" I hiss, tiny drops of spit spackle the back of the hand I use to grab his arm. "What the hell are you thinking? Smoking at a crime scene." I position my body to block any view that Jake and the D.A. might have if they glance through the picture window.

"Ease up, Maggie. I'll make sure I don't leave it behind. I'm not dumb." He looks at me with country singer eyes; eyes that can tell sad stories, make you feel the hurt, and want to climb into bed with him for a night of passion to soothe the pain.

Lee turns the video camera off, "Hear that Maggie? Nate ain't dumb. First thing they teach you, bring nothing into the scene, don't even pick yer nose, and here he is, hot shot himself, lighting up, but he says he ain't dumb."

I take the butt from his mouth, cup my hand underneath it and hurry to the bathroom. The toilet is thick with dust and tiny hairs are stuck to the seat. Brown fossilized stains stick to the bottom of the bowl. I try not to retch as I throw the butt in the rancid smelling water. I use the tip of my sandal to flush.

At age 24, Nate is the youngest detective on the force. He's the nephew of the Chief of Police, and the son of one of the township counsel members.

I lean close to him; the powdery residue of fingerprint dust tickles my nose. "I thought you loved being a cop." I whisper. The aroma of fried bacon sticks to his polo shirt.

"God, Maggie. I'm stressed, Okay?"

I roll my eyes. He lives with two rowdy roommates who've been cited several times for DUI but somehow the charges wind up underneath the political rug.

Nate is still built like the star linebacker he was at Penn State. His Jeep was bought and paid for by his wealthy family who also pay most of his household bills. Yet, Nate wants me to believe he is stressed.

"Can't get tickets to Dave Matthews? Oh, I know, the Taco Bell is going out of business, right?"

"No." He looks around the room. Lee has disappeared. Jake and the D.A. are still on the porch. It's just Nate and the dead, perverted, T-Ray Austin and me.

"I...uh...Maggie, you can't tell anyone this."

"Scout's honor," I raise my hand.

"I think I left my gun on the hood of my car when I left for the station this morning."

I grasp a handful of his shirt to keep from falling over. "What?"

"I got to the station and realized I didn't have my piece. I KNOW I took it with me when I left. I usually put my cup of coffee and the gun on top of the car while I unlock it."

"And you left them both on top of the hood when you drove away?"

"I remembered to take the coffee."

I study Nate's face closely. He is the consummate practical joker.

"If this is a prank," I warn him, "It's not funny."

"God, I wish it was."

Now I have the urge for nicotine and inhale deeply, trying to capture any remnants of cigarette smoke that remains.

Jake and the D.A. are no longer in front of the picture window.

"Are you sure you put it on top of your car?"

"Maggie, I called home and Fred went outside to look. He found my clip and some bullets in the middle of the road. Someone is walking around with my gun."

I make the sign of the cross. "I'll do what I can to help."

Jake steps into the house, blinking rapidly as his eyes adjust to interior light.

"How's it going in here?"

"Great," I smile. "I was just asking Nate what he thought about ol T-Ray here."

"What do you think Nate?" Jake steps around the corpse, tucking his notebook into his back pocket.

"I think it couldn't have happened to a more deserving person."

Nate clears his throat. "I gotta get back to dusting."

"Maggie...you want to take a walk through the house and see what you think?"

"Sure." I offer a reassuring glance in Nate's direction. He knows I have a soft spot for him.

I begin my walk through.

The inside of the house is much like the outside. Worn, uncared for. Grime clings to the television, the stereo. In the kitchen, a half eaten sandwich on the counter. Bologna on white. No dishes in the sink. Garbage can filled with paper plates, crumpled napkins, juice boxes. In the fridge; a half gallon of chocolate milk, the bologna, a package of chocolate covered graham crackers, and row upon row of root beer. In the cupboards; paper plates, potato chips, Doritos, Cheetos, a box of crackers and a can of cheese whiz. Junk food. Kid food.

Across from the kitchen is a small computer room; a laptop is open on the small desk.

"That bastard," I swear. "Jake, come here when you get a chance." I yell over my shoulder.

A screensaver of a dog chasing a cat fills the square monitor. My hand moves to the mouse and hovers over it. I know I shouldn't touch it. St. John, the Detective in charge of Computer Crimes, would spend ten minutes lecturing me on my mistake. Then he'd make me write a ten-page report on why I did what I did and post it in the Roll Call room.

I really didn't need to move the mouse. I knew what I would find.

T-Ray Austin had been in the middle of a trial, accused of molesting three boys on a baseball team. When T-Ray was initially arrested, a search of the house had turned up a computer loaded with thousands of pictures of child pornography. One of the conditions of his home surveillance was that he was not allowed to have a computer in the house.

Before I started my tour with the homicide unit, I had to spend four weeks with each department in order to understand how they worked with each other and what each department was responsible for. Robbery was a bit boring. Crime Scene was too technical, and the Special Victims Unit (formally known as Sex Crimes, but SVU is politically correct these days) was heartbreaking at best.

In the seven years I've been on the force, I know that if you put some Vicks Vapor rub into your nostrils, you could almost...almost...keep the smell of burnt flesh from making you sick. I've seen the legs of a man severed just above the knee after he fell into a machine at the tire plant. I've witnessed the decapitation of a motorcyclist; we had to search for ten minutes to find his head, it had rolled under thorn bushes that lined the road. I've seen the heartbreaking sight of a woman brutally raped and left for near dead; her body broken and covered with blood and her own vomit.

I'd been able to bury those visions deep within my mind. I packed up the emotion and dumped it on the side of a deserted road, knowing I might stumble upon it someday when I least wanted to. I could leave any images behind, with the exception of children who'd been abused. It didn't matter the method of abuse; sexually or physically…there was no place to abandon those pictures.

Sometimes I sneak into Zoey's room at night and watch her while she sleeps. I pray (and this is about the only time I do) to God, to Mary, to Jesus and ask that they please, please, please, watch over my little angel. I've watched the way her little mouth smiles while she dreams and I've actually wondered why I brought such an innocent, beautiful, person into a world filled with terror. Filled with people who wear the disguise of normalcy; gold cuff links, kind eyes, clean fingernails, perfect white teeth. Hiding under it all…the hideous fangs, the evil mind, lurking, waiting for a chance.

As a cop, a detective, I've seen wickedness, and it's not always the unshaven, beer chugging, tobacco spitting people. As a matter of fact, these people are usually guilty of the simplest crime; stupidity. Stealing to feed their family. Doing drugs to soften the rough edges of the world they live in. It's the person who you might be standing behind in a grocery line and you think to yourself, "This guy's got it together." What you don't know about the clean cut guy is that he is plotting to kill his wife for a life insurance payoff. He is robbing his employer blind so he can finance his addiction to massage parlors. That guy molests his own daughter. He threatens to kill her and her mother if she ever tells.

The years of wearing a badge have taught me that evil lives where it's least expected. No matter how well kept the garden, there are weeds that look like exotic flowers.

If only I could place some sort of magical netting over Zoey, something that would keep depraved people away from her. I could handle the falls, the bruises, the splinters…I could handle broken bones, a broken heart, sickness. All those things I could come to terms with. I could never handle Zoey being harmed by another human being.

Jake, Nate, and Lee crowd behind me.

"I thought he wasn't supposed to have a computer." Nate hisses.

"He wasn't. We confiscated his PC. We did a thorough search of his house and only found one. Someone must have brought this laptop in." Jake pushes my hand away from the mouse. "St. John will kill you if you touch it. Did you call him?"

"Not yet."

"Maybe we ought to think about refusing phone service and cable to prisoners who are electronically monitored in their homes." Nate offers.

I step out into the hall; the room suddenly feels polluted. "Yeah, I can just hear the ACLU screaming about the unfairness of that."

"Know what I think?" Lee's voice boomerangs off the walls, "I say fuck it. Let's do a half assed investigation. That way if we do get the guy who killed T-Ray, any defense attorney straight out of school could get the guy responsible for murdering this SOB off on a technicality." The anger in his voice is thick and hard.

Jake shakes his head, "I didn't hear that."

"Well, I did." Nate's voice comes from the pit of his gut; it's like strong coffee, wakes you right up with its heavy bite. "And while me and Lee don't always see eye to eye, I have to admit I ain't gonna lose any sleep over the dead guy on the living room floor. If he did that to any of my sister's kids...I'd have filled his body with bullet holes."

Jake looks at me, it's a look I know well. He wants me to recite the "We must uphold the law, we took an oath" speech that he has given me more times than he's bought me a drink. And we've spent at least two nights a month, for three years, in many a bar.

"Listen," I sigh, "as much as we think this guy should rot in hell, the fact is, he was murdered. As cops, it's our job to maintain the law. If we pick and choose which case we work hard at, we'd have more of a rotten reputation then we already do."

Lee sighs and picks up the video camera, "Thank God I'm retiring soon. You new guys are so fucking anal; you'd do a cavity search on your own mother."

"Whoa...Buddy," I hold up my hands, "That's Jake's philosophy. I agree with you two; I'm glad he's dead."

I want out of this place. My skin is starting to feel as if tiny bugs have crawled into my veins and are trying to burrow. I can't wait to get home to take a shower. "I'm going down the street to interview the old lady."

"I'll go with you." Jake follows. He looks over his shoulder and reminds Lee to call St. John to pick up the computer. Then he points at Nate, "Don't touch it. Don't turn it off; don't unplug it."

Nate holds his hands in the air as if surrendering.

When I walk by T.Ray's lifeless body, I have the urge to kick him. I settle for spitting on the lawn once we get outside.

"That's real lady like." Jake shakes his head.

"Who ever said I'm a lady?"

"Ain't that the truth," He puts an arm around my shoulders and hugs me close as we walk down the street.

Innocence is a flower which withers when touched, but blooms not again, though watered with tears.

—Hooper

I had no time to truly digest the fact that I had just killed someone. My life immediately went back to its daily routine. Every so often, I found myself remembering the look in his eyes as I pulled out the gun. The disbelief on his face and yet, there was also peacefulness. He looked at the gun, then into my eyes, as if he had been waiting for this. Perhaps hoping for it. He didn't say a word, though there wasn't really time to protest or ask why.

You may think that I must have been molested as a child. I wasn't. I had the most idyllic childhood imaginable. Better than the Brady Bunch because my parents were never divorced, never even fought. They kept reins on us, letting them stretch just enough to let us make our own choices. Perhaps we didn't always make the right decision, but they always caught us just before we hit the ground.

I was never molested but I'd had two close calls.

The first incident occurred the summer my sister and I were allowed to bike to the community pool without my mother. Grace was ten. I was eight. She thought I was her slave. I had to carry the wet towels and swimsuits tucked under my arm because she was in charge of the money mom had given us to buy a snack on the way home. If I didn't do as my sister demanded, I could forget the double scoop of mint chocolate ice cream from the Dairy Barn.

As soon as we pulled our Schwinns out of the bike rack, I had the urge to throw her crap on the ground. If I cut through the basketball court and looped around the tennis court, I could be home ten minutes faster than Grace. I could forgo the Dairy Barn *because I had hid the last Nutty Buddy behind the box of frozen lima beans. Granted, it was nothing close to mint chocolate chip ice cream, but I wasn't so sure hauling all the shit was worth it.*

Of course, mom would ground me for a week because I left my sister behind which was a cardinal sin according to my mother. I'd have to stay home for seven days doing extra chores like moving all the knickknacks and dusting, even though the spots where the knickknacks had been resting were already clean.

There we were, pedaling side by side. My eyes sore from chlorine and sunshine. The muscles in my legs felt like lead balls, groaning in protest and working harder than they had in the pool.

He was sitting against a tree, staring at us. Hands in his lap. The only reason he caught my eye was because he had long hair the color of fresh school paper. His skin resembled leather.

"I got something for you, come over here." He laughed and waved something he was holding in his lap.

It was everything our mother had prepared us for. "Never get in a car with a stranger. If you get in a car with a stranger, it will be the last time anyone will ever see you alive." "Never listen to a man or woman who offers you candy, money, or toys." "Never open our door for a stranger. Never answer the phone when you're home alone. Never help anyone search for their dog or cat, and never give directions to a stranger." She was like a broken record, once a week admonishing us on the evil that lurked right around the corner, waiting to prey on us like a hungry alligator.

Grace and I would roll our eyes as soon as she turned her back. Sometimes Grace would sneak into my room after lights out, creeping along the walls, her body casting a tall, thin shadow. "Little kid, I have a present for you." She'd whisper in a creepy, deep voice.

"Is it a big present or a little present?" I'd have to bite down on a corner of my pillow so I wouldn't laugh out loud, alerting our parents that we were not fast asleep.

"It's a big present, just for you little one." She'd snarl, jump on my body and I'd whisper, "Get off me you pervert or I'll tell my mother and she'll beat your head with a frying pan!"

We'd laugh quietly until our stomachs felt like they did when we had to do a hundred sit-ups in Mr. Snow's gym class. Then she'd tiptoe back to her room.

"What does he have?" I asked my sister, steering my bike so close to hers our front tires almost collided.

We squinted against the sunshine and the realization of what the man was holding in his hand hit us at the same time because we gasped long and loud.

"It's His Dick." Grace looked at me, her eyes ignited with alarm and disbelief.

I couldn't take my eyes off the extended limb he was rubbing; it reminded me of a giant night crawler. My legs automatically lifted my body up and started pedaling furiously, all the while staring at the man. Not because I was fascinated, but to make sure he didn't run after us, his penis bobbing in the air while he lunged at our bikes with wide, monster, hairy, arms.

It took only a minute to clear the park but it seemed like an hour. We pedaled in silence for three blocks; the only sound I could hear was the blood rushing in my ears, the air whizzing in and out of our tire spokes. When we got to the Getty Gas Station, Grace slowed to a stop and shook her head. "That was disgusting." She spit on the blacktop; her bangs were wet and smashed against her forehead.

One of the station attendants was pumping gas for a convertible. He took off his cap and repositioned it backwards, a small tuft of black hair popping thru the hole.

"Maybe we should tell someone." I imagined confiding in the lanky boy; sitting on the orange chairs in the gas station while he called the cops. Listening to Grace as she told the story to a sweaty, cranky cop. And knowing Grace, the story would change from a man sitting against the tree rubbing himself to a naked man who had chased us, screaming the "f" word at the top of his lungs.

"That creep is gone by now. He'd be really stupid to stay there with his…his…" I could barely bring myself to say it.

Grace scrunched up her mouth like she'd just swallowed sour milk, "His dick waving in the air."

The boy glanced at us, wiped his brow with the back of his hand, then turned back to watch the numbers on the gas tank roll by. Ping. Ping. Ping.

"We can't tell mom." Grace shook her head furiously; damp strands of hair whipped her cheeks.

I agreed. Mom would never let us come back to the pool alone. She'd insist on coming with us and that would mean we would only go once or twice a week because she couldn't miss her soap operas, or making sun tea, or vacuuming.

It was at least a week before we went back. In the pool, with the silver fence that surrounded it, we felt protected. We splashed around and pretended to drown each other, see who could hold their breath the longest. But every time we passed the tree on the way home, we remembered.

Two years later, at the small park down the street from my house, I was practicing my lay-ups because basketball tryouts were a week away. I was alone. I didn't want anyone to know what I was doing in case I embarrassed myself and didn't make the team.

It had just rained and worms were still inching their way over the black top. The rain had kept everyone inside, and the worms and I were the only ones in the park. I was kicking them (very gently) to the side of the court when a gray haired man with droopy jeans appeared at the edge of the court. He smelled like a marsh at low tide, and like my dad after his office Christmas party.

"Hey, kid." He had thick eyebrows that grew together.

An uneasy feeling grabbed at my gut. I backed away; stepping on a translucent worm. I felt it squish under my shoe. The macaroni and cheese I'd had for lunch lunged into my throat; it lumped itself there until I swallowed and the noodles wiggled back to my stomach.

"Hi," it was my voice, though I didn't recall giving it permission to speak. It had something to do with manners and respect to my elders; no matter how stinky or strange looking they were. No matter how much my mother had warned me.

"Are you interested in making a few extra dollars? Say, ten bucks?"

I didn't say anything. Only clutched the orange ball to my chest, feeling the small bumps on the ball press into the fleshy part of my forearms.

"I clean the park." He smiled, "I pick up litter and stuff. I really don't feel like cleaning the bathroom. If you'd help me out, say do the mirrors while I clean the floor, I'd be happy to give you some money."

I started to back away.

One. I'd been coming to this park since I was little and had never ever seen this man, nor any man pick up the stray candy wrappers. And men in yellow shirts and blue pants always mowed the park. I was at least smart enough to realize that.

Two. This guy didn't have any cleaning supplies. No buckets, mops, not even a rag hanging out of his pocket.

My legs spun. The park exit was twenty steps away. I reached the road so quickly I thought maybe I should try out for the track team. I felt protected by the cars parked along the curb; the homes that squatted on perfect squares of grass. I glanced back every few minutes. But the man was nowhere in sight. It wasn't until I reached home that I realized my hands were empty. I had dropped the ball when I started to run, hadn't even realized I'd let it go.

I never told anyone about what happened, thinking I may have overreacted. And I never did try out for the basketball team.

Detective Bennigan
August 2, Friday. Afternoon

It takes three jabs at the doorbell and repeated pounding on the door to alert the little old lady that eventually shuffles to the door. She is dressed in pink. Pink shirt, pink polyester pants, pink slippers. Even her hollow cheeks are pink.

"Oh, hello," she peers through the screen. "Are you the new Meals On Wheels people?"

"Uh, no, we're detectives with the North Twilight police department. We wanted to ask you a few questions." Jake offers her a wide smile.

She purses her chapped lips as if she is going to whistle; her white eyebrows knit together. "Sure you are. And I'm the Easter Bunny."

She may not be the Easter Bunny, but she could easily be the mother of the Easter Bunny. She looks like a piece of bubble gum, but the smell coming through the screen is a mixture of menthol cream and peppermints.

"Miss," Jake fishes his badge out of his pocket. "I'm Detective Jake Buchanan and this is Detective Maggie Bennigan. There's been a crime in the neighborhood, and we'd like to ask you some questions."

She shakes her head, thin wisps of fragile hair tremble in the air. "I watch Oprah. I know about this scam. You'll get in my house, beat me, and steal all my china."

"We don't need to enter your home. We can ask you some questions standing right here, if that will make you happy."

"Do you have a search warrant?" She smacks her lips together, her eyes narrowing until they almost disappear into her sockets.

"Pardon?" Jake asks.

"A Search Warrant. I watch NYPD Blue. And Third Watch."

I shift my stance and glance away, trying hard to stifle the laughter trying desperately to force its way out.

"Okay…hmmm. Well, we don't need a search warrant to ask you a few questions. A search warrant would be if we wanted to search your house; if we thought you'd committed a crime or something."

"What kind of crime do you think I committed?" She folds paper thin arms across a brittle chest.

Jake looks at me. "This isn't going to work. Maybe we should have some uniforms come down to talk to her."

"I can hear you. Just because I'm old doesn't mean I can't hear, especially when you're standing right in front of me."

I notice the flush begin to creep into Jake's cheeks. Never a good sign.

"Here's the deal. If you can look out one of the windows, up the street, you'll see our police cars. There's been a murder and we need…"

She pushes the screen door open so swiftly Jake has to hop down one step to prevent his face from being flattened.

"A murder!" She clacks her dentures.

She shuffles out to the edge of the porch and stares up the street. "Holy Hot Cross Buns! If I could whistle, I would." She squints hard, her eyes turning into raisins. "Who got it?"

"Ummm, Terrance Ray Austin." Jake flips open his notepad.

"He's the sicko, isn't he? The pervert?"

We nod.

"Well, good, he deserves everything he got. Did you see his lawn? Shameful."

"Did you notice anything unusual today, Mrs…?"

"Mrs. Jasper." The door creaks as she opens it again and steps inside. "What is this world coming to? I can't wait till God takes me. I try not to complain so much about life, because the more you complain, the longer he leaves you on this earth. But…" She shakes her head, "Men taking liberties with children, kids being stolen right from their own beds. Old people being beaten and robbed. No one has respect anymore. No one."

"Did you see or hear anything unusual today?"

"No. I was in the back of the house most of the morning, watching my shows."

Her voice has become tired as she talks to us through the screen. She reminds me of my own grandmother, who passed away when I was 28. Grandma Kate was a chain smoking, one shot of bourbon before bed, read the daily paper while making disapproving clicks with her tongue, kind of woman. She always made sure I felt loved by stuffing me with homemade nut roll, bread, meatloaf, and the tenderest roast I've tried to duplicate but failed miserably.

"I went to put the laundry out on the line and a very handsome, sweaty man told me he had to use the phone because he found a dead body."

"So, you let a stranger use your phone but you won't let two detectives ask you a few questions?" Jake teases her kindly.

"I was outside. He was cute. Darling eyes. The cat's pajamas." Her fire has returned.

"Meow," I whisper.

"I heard that." Mrs. Jasper secures the latch on the door. "I didn't actually believe that fella when he'd said he found a dead body. Thought he just needed to make a phone call." She adjusts her dentures with her tongue. "I need you to leave now. General Hospital is about to come on."

"Mrs. Jasper!" I call after the departing pink fluff, pressing my nose against the scratchy screen.

"Have you noticed anything unusual the past few days? People or cars that you didn't recognize?"

She is slowly making her way across a darkened sitting room. She waves a hand in the air. "Come see me tomorrow, after 4 and before 5." She tells us before pushing through a wooden door and disappearing behind it.

"Oh God," Jake shakes his head and retreats down the steps, "I need a drink."

"We have so many possible suspects to rule out." I feel my brain begin to cluster and tighten in my skull.

It is usually just the opposite, too few suspects, but the list of people who hate T-Ray Austin will have us running all over town. And it's way past my lunchtime. I'm jonesing for a ham hoagie from Slack's Hoagie Shack.

"Could be a quick case, we find this guy within a day or two. I have a good feeling. Open and Shut." Jake snaps his fingers.

"All I know is, I was supposed to have a fun, relaxing time tonight." I complain. "Becky and I were going to the Tex Mex. I thought I might even find someone to smooth the wrinkles in my sheets, if you know what I mean."

He rolls his eyes, "Tell you what, we put in some really good leg work on this case, and I'll buy you the first round of drinks tomorrow night."

"You think Lucy will let you out of the house?"

"I think Lucy will be kicking me out of the house. Every five minutes I ask her how she is. She yells at me, telling me to shut up, she'll let me know when it's time."

"Becky is gonna be pissed I can't go out tonight. I'm pissed too."

"Why are you pissed? What's the big deal if you go out tomorrow instead of tonight?"

"Because I have to search for someone who killed a pervert. And, quite frankly, I'm glad he's dead."

"Maggie. C'mon. Don't say that."

I put a hand on Jake's arm and turn him around until he's looking into my eyes. "Jake, now that you're going to be a parent...can't you understand..." I glance up at the grimy windows in T-Ray's house. "If we never catch this killer, would you honestly care?"

Jake lowers his head and kicks the sidewalk with his scuffed sneaker. "I can't judge, Maggie. If I did, I'd never be able to do my job. If I let my emotions take over, I'd be worthless. I want to be the best at everything I do. You know that. Anger and hate cloud rational thinking."

I cross my arms. "Jake, there is nothing rational about a man who forces children to have sex with him."

"Look, Mags, I can't explain, okay. Emotion works for you. It drives you. You can work with it. I can't. It would ruin me."

"Fine, maybe you should be working for the ACLU. Rights for everyone. Even those who don't deserve them."

"C'mon Maggie, I always respect your opinions; you should respect mine."

"What?" I laugh bitterly. I'm not sure when or where this anger attached itself to me, but it's overwhelming and because Jake is standing in my line of vision...

"You don't respect my opinions. You're always too busy telling everyone how to do their job. We can't all be as perfect as you. You were anal to begin with, but now that your wife is going to have a baby, you've progressed from anal to a big, fat, piece of shit."

Jake's face is emotionless but shadows of hurt darken his eyes. I can't believe the words I've said, and as usual, wish I would have thought before opening my mouth.

"I'm sorry," I offer a weak apology that he waves away. "It's hot out, I'm hungry, I haven't has sex since..."

"The Dentist."

"Doesn't count."

"Well, I can't help you with the horny part," Jake shrugs, the clouds of hurt dissipating as fast as they had arrived, "but...how bout I take you to Slack's Hoagie Shack and buy you lunch."

My anger left as quickly as it had arrived. It's amazing what the promise of meat and cheese between a roll can do to me.

Every man has the right to risk his own life in order to preserve it. Has it ever been said that a man who throws himself out the window to escape from a fire is guilty of suicide?

—*Jean-Jacques Rousseau*

The sky is gray, pregnant with rain. Cranky winds whip the dust and litter in the street, creating tiny twisters filled with gravel, silver gum wrappers, and dirt.

I duck into Agatha's Cyber Café to wait out the storm that will no doubt begin any minute.

Freshly brewed coffee and the sweet smell of chocolate chip cookies wraps around me, like a hug from a good friend. The walls are the color of coffee, rich with cream. Pictures of French bakeries and restaurants are hung here and there inviting closer inspection.

I slide in a chair with a cup of hazelnut coffee. I uncurl the morning paper tucked under my arm, spread it across the wobbly table. The headline jumps at me; "Alleged Child Molester Murdered."

Warmth spreads up my neck, under my chin, across my cheeks. I feel like there is an arrow above my head pointing down at me, fluorescent and throbbing with accusation. **KILLER.** *Surely, everyone must be staring at me. But the few people in the café are either drumming away on the laptops chained to the tables, or staring out the windows, waiting for the relief of rain we've so desperately needed this summer.*

I take a deep breath, pressing my back against the chair. The article is short, not even mentioning how T-Ray was killed and ends with the sentence: "The police are working on several leads."

A small smile works its way across my face. Of course the police would have several leads. Starting with every family that T-Ray Austin plagued by defiling their children. I take a sip of my coffee; feel the muscles that had been so tense begin to melt.

I reread the article a few more times, as if to burn the words into my head. And then it becomes this to me: I feel as if I am reading it as if I had not been there. I am nothing more than the average person who is reading the paper, learning of the murder for the first time.

After I feel reassured, calm, I scan the rest of the paper. There, on page two, is an article about a man who was arrested after meeting a young boy online and arranging a meeting with him. When the boy met "Charles Wentworth" outside the mall, Mr. Wentworth asked the boy to perform oral sex on him, at which point, the twelve year old boy jumped out of the car and alerted a security guard. Though he may have not been all that smart when agreeing to meet someone he met in a chat room, he was smart enough to get the license plate number as he escaped. Charles Wentworth is now being held in lieu of ten thousand dollars. And Charles Wentworth is a convicted molester, who had been paroled less than a year ago, after spending five years in prison.

The coffee begins to somersault in my gut. It just doesn't end, men who prey on children. And the court system…well, how many molesters spend time in the slammer, only to be released into the world with the same thoughts and longings? They should drive them straight from prison to a playground and toss them out with a bag of candy and a video camera. Throwing a sexual predator back into society is like putting an obese woman who's been on a liquid diet for two months into a bakery and telling her not to touch anything.

There is a titter of voices around me, pulling me away from the paper. I lift my head. People have gathered in front of the windows, pressed hands on the glass, their mouths curved up in delight. Rain, fat and heavy, falls from the sky. It has been such a dry summer. It will not last, this rain. And it won't erase the damage that has been done; it won't revive dead flowerbeds, it won't soften baseball fields that are harder than concrete. The rain has come too late; there is no turning back.

Detective Bennigan
August 3, Saturday. Night

The Tex Mex is in full swing. I'm exhausted, but as soon as I enter the bar, a second wind fills my sails. The Tex Mex does that. The walls are mango and teal. A mural of a Mexican village, painted by one of the regulars, decorates part of the ceiling. The crowd is as salty and diverse as the margaritas they serve. Construction workers sit beside business owners. Lawyers mingle with sales girls from Macy's. It's one of the reasons I love it. Variety is the spice of life. No one is ever out of place at the Tex Mex. There's always a niche to fall into.

The margaritas here are more potent then any illegal drug. The house limit is three. One margarita could make a nun flirt shamelessly with a Priest. Two margaritas and she'll be locking lips with the Priest. Three margaritas and she'll be doing a slow strip tease on top of the bar, bouncing her boobs in time to the music.

"You sure you'd rather not be at home, sleeping?" Becky asks. She sits to my left. Jake kept his promise and sits on my right.

"No, I've been dying to go out for weeks now. And besides, I felt like shit bagging out on you last night." I dig through the basket of snack mix, in search of pretzel nibs.

"If I got ditched last night because some asshole got himself murdered, who am I to complain?" Becky shrugs, her blonde hair gently sloping over her exposed tan shoulders.

Becky wasn't the only person who was thrilled that T-Ray Austin was dead. Every person that Jake and I interviewed had been overjoyed to hear he was no longer on this earth. They all co-operated, most offered us food (Clayton Weller and his wife make the best barbecue on the East Coast). The men shook our hands when we left and three mothers hugged us as if we were family.

"Anyone?" Jake had asked as we finished our last interview at two this afternoon.

"You're kidding, right? Mr. Peters is about the only guy who qualifies as somewhat suspicious and only because his alibi was somewhat vague. Was he at the mall? Grocery store? Dry cleaners? Couldn't pin down the time...and he was red in the face and kept running his hand over his chin."

"I bet he was banging someone at one of those posh hotels right around the corner from his law firm in Philly. Probably his secretary. As long as it checks out he was at work, before and after the time of death, we can forget about him."

"Nah, we can forget about him anyway. I didn't have any sort of feeling about him. Anyone else for that matter."

"No sudden pulse accelerations?"

"Nope. None. As happy as these parents were to learn T-Ray bit the big one, there wasn't one person I could even fathom as a suspect."

We had been outside the station, sitting in the car, the air conditioner cranked all the way. A brief storm had cooled the air from a blistering 100 degrees to a roasting 92 degrees. The air conditioner in our offices had blown last week. Jake and I had grown accustomed to car conferences.

"These parents are all...oh, I don't know...apple pie, coupon clipping, throw the milk out a day before expiration, kinda people. I don't see any of them capable of murder." I had told him.

"Yeah, but it's their kids we're talking about. T-Ray hurt those kids in a way no parent can accept. What he did was intentional and sick. What he did is something that could make a coupon clipping, apple pie baking, mother go over the edge."

"That's the key right there. If one of the parents became so enraged that they took a gun and killed someone at point blank range, they wouldn't be acting rationally. They would have done it out in the open...not caring who was around. When we interviewed them, they would have cracked under pressure, they would have given something away. Even if someone hired a hit man to take T-Ray out...I don't think there was one parent we talked to that could act so detached, so calm. There were no red flags."

Jake ran his hand around the steering wheel. "I keep thinking we're missing something. Maybe the lawyer from Philly will turn up to be guilty of something other than having an affair."

"Maybe, but I don't feel it." At that point I'd been awake 24 hours and couldn't wait to get home for the nap I so desperately needed. We had nothing to show for our time, other than overtired nerves and bags under our eyes that were so big, you could call them suitcases.

"Oh God, look what the heavens have offered us." Becky pinches the back of my hand, tipping her head toward the front door of the bar.

"Luke Foreman." I sigh.

Jake groans.

"And he's alone." Becky whispers.

I take a long sip of my margarita and try not to make it too obvious that I am following his every move.

Luke Forman is all muscle and almost as tall as a doorway. Even a wrestler from the WWE would think twice before pissing him off. His brown eyes, however, are soft, warm, and can melt someone as cold as Hilary Clinton.

A low growl emanates from Jake. Five years ago, Jake had been recruited by the FBI to work an undercover stint that lasted for three months in NJ. Mafia, drugs, and arms dealing were involved. Luke had brought Jake in as his 'cousin'. Other than the fact the guys they wanted to put behind bars are now wearing jumpsuits and making license plates, Jake refuses to tell me anything more. He tenses every time Luke is around, though Luke seems to hold no animosity toward Jake.

I try my best to keep my eyes focused everywhere he wasn't. On the bar, on Becky's gold wedding band that I'd helped Marty pick out, on the lights above the bar that had muddled after just three sips of my drink.

Becky was now pinching the fleshy part just above my knee. It was a habit of excitement that carried over from our junior high days. "He's coming." She giggles.

"Detective Bennigan." His voice is warm in my ear.

"Agent Foreman." I lean back and smile, trying very hard not to appear eager.

Luke Foreman usually had a woman on his arm. Not just any woman, but one who could have walked right off a magazine cover; thin as thread with hollow hungry eyes.

"You remember Becky?" I grab her arm and squeeze. It was a firm reminder…don't mess this up. Don't mention that my house is always full of dirty clothes and dishes. Don't mention that I wear plaid sweats to bed and my ex-husbands hole ridden t-shirts. Don't bring up the fact that I'm desperate to feel the warmth of a real mans body beside me, over me, under me or anywhere near me.

"Yes, we met last year I think. Maggie brought you to the F.O.P picnic."

"And you were a speaker there. Held everybody's attention, if I remember correctly."

From the other side of me, Jake laughs.

"Sure, he held everyone's attention after three hours of non stop drinking."

"How have you been, Jake? Are you a daddy yet?" Luke holds out his hand, winking at me.

"Any day now." Jake lifts the bottle of Corona to his mouth and stares straight ahead.

"I read about the murder in the paper today. You guys working that?" Luke is standing so close to me, I can practically feel the rise and fall of his chest.

"Yeah, we got pinned on it. Stu and Chet are still working on that body of the woman found in Shriner's Creek." I feel a slow warmth flood my body.

"Any leads yet?"

"Do you think we'd actually be talking about it here?" Jake snaps, his coldness wrapping around the barstools.

"You know, I think I'm gonna play the juke box." I glance at Becky, "You want to join me?" I grab a dollar bill from the pile of money we had stacked on the bar, agreeing we would leave once there was only a twenty dollar bill left, enough for a tip.

"Nah. This drink has me tanked already. Best if I keep my butt glued to the bar. Wouldn't want to trip and have to spend time in the emergency room when I could be spending time here." She looks up at Luke, raising her eyebrows up and down so quickly, I thought they would shoot off her head. An oh so subtle hint.

"I'll go with you." Luke laughs and puts his hand on my elbow.

With Luke directly behind me, I don't have to fight my way through the crowd. They glance up and step aside with respect.

A battle of voices ensues in my head. There is the rational Maggie, "Forget him. He's Fed. It'd never work out. Remember your promise to yourself. Never sleep with another cop."

There is the horny Maggie, "But he's a Fed. Technically, he's not a cop. Doesn't count."

"One in the same. He lives across the street from the bar. You see him almost every time you're here. And what if you slept with him and it was terrible? What if he laughs at your boobs."

"Oh God. No one has ever laughed at my boobs. He's not that type of guy. He has manners. He's charming. Charming men don't point out flaws. At least not right away. And I love my boobs. Even if they are a bit susceptible to gravitational forces."

"What if it's great but then he never calls you again and the next time you see him, he's got another emaciated woman hanging on his arm."

"All I want is one night of hot sex. It's been so long. I don't even want a relationship."

"Liar."

"Maggie?" Luke looks down at me, we are now standing in front of the jukebox; it hangs on the wall and I know the selections by heart. I've tried desperately to get the manager to change the music, but to no avail. I once arrested him for DUI and he obviously held this against me. The Rolling Stones, Pink Floyd, Stevie Nicks, music that would be enjoyed while smoking a doobie, occupies most of the selections. "Maggie?" He says again.

I look up at him. God, if he kissed me right now I'd die a very happy woman.

"Did you say something? Your lips were moving, but no words were coming out."

"Oh, just, uh, talking to myself." I laugh nervously.

"So, what do you think?" He leans against the wall as I press the glowing red square to flip through the selections.

"About?" I refuse to glance up at him, too afraid he'd be able to read what my eyes are thinking.

"About…Hmm, the Phillies?"

"I don't like baseball. Too slow. And they get too much money. Old baseball was good, though; Tug McGraw, Catfish Hunter, Shoeless Joe. I like hockey; it's a tough sport. All that body slamming against the boards."

"I have season tickets to the Flyers. Maybe if you play Garth Brooks I'll take you to a game."

My eyes widen, though I'm still staring at the CD's that I'm whipping through. I can't bring myself to meet his gaze yet. "You like country music?"

I can see his reflection in the jukebox. He shrugs, and then that smile, slow and sweet as molasses, curves round his mouth. "Country's okay, but I seem to remember one time I was here and you played Garth Brooks. Friends In Low Places, I believe it was."

I take a deep breath, press the button and watch as the selections flip, flip, flip, until I land on Garth Brooks. It isn't really a Garth crowd tonight. The crowd is rather young; college types with tight shirts. Friends In Low Places is usually a song for the early happy hour crowd on a Friday. Older, construction guys, or businessmen, who've moved beyond trying to impress people with the fad music of the moment, preferring music with spirit, soul.

I punch in the code for Garth. 2107.

"Okay, now you have to take me to a Flyers game. Next."

"What do you think about fireworks?"

"I love them, but unless I can see them from my house, it's a waste." "Why's that?"

"Because my mom used to take us to see fireworks when we were little. We'd have to hike ten minutes to find a spot to put our blanket. Then we'd have to wait another thirty minutes until it got dark. Then we'd ooohh and ahhh for twenty minutes. After it was over, we'd have to fight our way back to the car. Another fifteen minutes. Then we'd have to wait in a traffic jam for close to an hour. Just not worth it."

"So I shouldn't ask you to go see any fireworks?"

The selections whir by, making a slapping noise as the selections I don't like land on top of each other.

I hate head games. I hate to play them; I dislike it even more when I'm on the receiving end. Did he want to take me out or didn't he?

"How about Counting Crows? Murder of One?" I punch in the code before he has a chance to answer.

"Murder of One. That would be a good newspaper headline. Murder of One."

"You're right." I press the square again. The CD's flash by quickly. Garth has begun to play, and I look up at the crowd, trying to gauge their expressions.

One lone woman, dressed in a white tank top, boobs heavy with age, lips cracked with orange lipstick, rolls her shoulders in time with the beat.

"So, no fireworks?"

I search for Tom Petty. Though he was popular when I was in school, he still seems to be a favorite of every age group.

"What happened to the last girl you were dating?" There's my big mouth again.

"She went back to Sweden. Hated the hot weather. And the cheesesteaks were making her fat. I think she was a size one by the time she left."

"Wow, how horrible for her." I look over my shoulder. Our eyes lock and hold.

"Okay, if you don't want to go see fireworks with me, what do you want to do?"

Oh, I but I was seeing fireworks…right there in his eyes. I was feeling sparks between my legs.

I bite my lip in order to suppress the giggle that has floated to my lips like bubbles to the top of a champagne flute. "Let's just see how this night goes, and take it from there." God, if only I were as cool as I sounded.

"Maggie." A familiar male voice douses the flames that are starting to spread like wildfire.

I turn, and there is Nate, blood shot eyes. His breath smells as if he's smoked a whole carton of cigarettes.

"Hey Nate," Luke offers his hand.

They shake. Nate asks if he can see me outside.

Luke leans over and whispers, "I'll go talk to Becky, make sure she doesn't fall off the barstool." Each word tickles my ear from the inside out.

"This better be good." I murmur as I follow Nate outside.

The air outside is still hot and sticky, yet feels refreshing after inhaling second hand smoke for the better part of an hour.

"I had to report it." He leans against his Jeep. Shoves his hands deep into his jean shorts. I have never seen him so serious, or sad.

"I told Lt. Schaffer. He fucking freaked out man." Nate shakes his head from side to side. "He had to call Andy."

Andy is Nate's uncle, Chief Hightower.

"And?" I nudge him on.

"And they had to suspend me. Jesus. I fucked up." He wipes his nose with the back of his hand.

"How long?"

Nate and I have had a big sister/little brother relationship since he started. He'd come to me when he had questions; on procedures, how to woo a woman to his bed, how to break up with her when it didn't work out, how to get through a shift when he was hung over. We've spent a few drunken nights in his Jeep, talking after the bars had closed and neither of us wanted to call it quits.

We've confided in each other, how we both felt like no matter where we went, or what we did, we always seemed to be the outsiders. And we seemed to get only so far until a swift kick in the ass sent us right back to Start. Me with my divorce and Nate never really feeling like part of the department because of his family connections. Other cops had a hard time taking him seriously. We both worried we'd never find that great love. That Jerry MaGuire, Moulin Rouge, Serendipity, Someone Like You, love story.

"It's complicated…the suspension. Because of this murder, they don't want to pull me off of what I started."

"You're our best fingerprint guy." I tell him, and I mean it.

He shrugs. "They said a few days. Do some follow up work on it quietly. My pay is suspended. Said they had to do it in case it got out in the papers. That way they can look like they took it seriously. And they did take it seriously. Jesus. I've never seen my dad so pissed, or Andy, for that matter. Thought all the buttons were gonna fly right off his shirt while he was bawling me out."

We share a smile at the image of barrel gutted Andy losing his shirt.

The back door of the bar opens, hazy light spills out to the parking lot. A bitter faced Jake emerges.

"Christ." Nate groans.

Gravel crunches under Jake's shoes.

"You leaving already?" I ask.

"I'm not sticking around to listen to Luke's stories all night." Jake looks at Nate.

"So…ya got a few days off."

Nate pulls himself up, shoulders back, as if getting ready for a series of head blows.

"You heard?" Nate's voice is flat, defeated.

"I overheard you tell Maggie you lost your gun yesterday." Jake tells us matter of factly.

"What?" Nate and I cry.

"Why didn't you say anything to me?" I put my hand on the hood of the Jeep to keep from falling over, the balance of my world is slightly off kilter.

Jake shrugs. "Cause I overheard it. You didn't tell me, Nate didn't tell me. It was none of my business."

Just when I'm ready to give up on Jake, he gives a glimpse of compassion.

"We all make mistakes." He shrugs again. "Nate doesn't need his nose rubbed in it. I knew he'd do the right thing."

This is why I love Jake.

Nate deflates like a tire punctured with a knife. "Jesus, Jake. Thanks."

"I'm gonna be getting home. Why don't you two go back in, have a good time. It'll work itself out Nate, don't do anything stupid tonight." Jake cocks his head toward the bar. He pulls his keys out of his pocket.

I throw my arms around him, hugging him. He pulls away, embarrassed at my display of affection.

"Maggie?" He grabs my shoulders and stares into my eyes.

"Yes?"

"I know you're horny and all, but, could you please not go home with the F.B.I agent?"

This is why I hate Jake.

"I'm outta here, I'll see you in the bar Maggie." Nate slaps Jake on the back. "And thanks again Jake."

We wait until the back door swallows him and then I push Jake's hands away.

"Can you give me one good reason, Jake?"

Jake looks up to the sky.

"Is he a dirty Fed or something?"

"No."

"Well, what then? Something happened in Jersey, is that it?"

Jake searches the sky. "Full moon."

"C'mon Jake."

"Can't you just trust me, Maggie? For once in your life. Trust me."

"Can't you trust me, Jake? Can't you trust me to make the right decisions?"

And there it is, the scar on my knee that is almost healed, and then…WHAM, something tears it off. He will forever be my teacher. I will always be the apprentice. I will try to win his approval and never quite manage to do it.

He starts to walk to his car. I have to run to keep up with his strides.

"Jake? Jake!"

He climbs in the car, rolls the window halfway down. My fingers curl over the top of the glass.

"Maggie, I'm not the one that questions the choices you make. I'm not the one that doesn't trust your instincts…you're the one who doubts everything you do." His voice is soft, but I feel as if my hand has been burned and I quickly pull it away.

Chance is always powerful. Let your hook be always cast; in the pool where you least expect it, there will be a fish.

—Ovid

Sometimes, inspiration comes looking for you.

I had been ready to leave Agatha's Cyber Café when something stopped my hand from pushing the door open and stepping out into the rain. It was the methodical tapping of fingers on the computer, reaching up and tugging at my ears. The rolled newspaper under my arm was spreading warmth through my chest.

I walked back to the counter, dug out my drivers license, and the teenage girl with blonde braids and strawberry breath dropped a piece of paper with an access code written on it into my outstretched hand.

I sat in front of the computer, and watched as my clammy fingers went to work.

I found a chat room titled "Home Alone".

I used the screen name "Phillyfan90"

"hey wht up" I typed.

A few acknowledgements.

"I'm bored rainin here" My words flashed.

"Whr u from?" Yankfan1 asked.

"PA. phillies getit?"

The conversation went on about baseball for a few minutes, then Yankfan1 asked me to join him in a private chat.

"See any games this year?" He asked.

"nah my moms always working" I added a frown face.

"Dad can take u?"

"don't see him." I typed back.

"I can get u tickets to game!"

"REALLY" I add smiley face.

"I can drive to PA, I'm only 3 hours away."

I glance around the café. A couple in the corner are holding hands and smiling at each other. Two grandmas are cackling over cheesecake and coffee. A smart dressed woman has a cell phone pressed to her ear.

"Kool" I type back.

"Can I take pictre of you? I swear I'll show no one."

The blood in my veins rushes to my heart, overwhelming it; I worry it will crack my ribs. Could it be THIS EASY?

"don't know" I type back.

"No presre."

"What if you just show me your privates? I won't tuch. Then you can hva tikets and 25 dollars."

I wait a moment. First to catch my breath. Second, I don't want to seem too eager.

"Phillyfan?"

"where at?" I finally answer.

"Mall close to you?"

"yeh...but...I know park no one goes to beter there."

"K. But, this is between u and me, K? I can get you more stuff later." He adds big smiley face.

"K."

"Where is park?"

I hesitate. If I give him street directions, he may wonder how a 12 year old is so familiar with names of streets.

"its called whistle stop park not sure how exactly how to tell you to get there."

"Is it by anything?"

"its off of countyline road I know that not too far from the Walmart."

"I'll find it. How will u get there?"

"walk" I have stopped breathing.

"Can u meet me at 9 tonight?" Yankfan1 types.

"yea."

"CU there"

"cu" I log off.

It isn't until I've walked a few blocks that I realize it has stopped raining. The sun is back in its perch.

Detective Bennigan
August 4, Sunday.

I wake up with a head the size of a football and a mouth that feels caked with dust. OH NO. I'm afraid to open my eyes. Bits and pieces of last night sew themselves together like patches of a quilt until it unfolds in my mind and I remember it all.

The Tex Mex. Jake. Nate. Becky singing karaoke only there was no karaoke machine. Nate repeating over and over, "Jake is the best, isn't he?"

And then there was Luke.

I sit upright; lighting strikes behind my eyes. I slowly lay back down. These are not my pillows. These blue sheets are not mine. The floor is not littered with dirty clothes. It is not my room.

I remember vaguely…Luke told me I was too drunk to drive home. He walked me across the street, practically carried me up the porch of his Victorian house.

"Oh this is so pretttttyyy." I had slurred as he helped me inside and led me to the bedroom.

"It's so clean!" I started clapping.

"Thanks." He had laughed, peeled back the covers and helped me climb in.

"Shouldn't we take off our clothes first?" I had giggled.

He had rested his body next to mine and kissed me. A long, slow, kiss that drew my breath from my body straight into his. I wasn't sure if the room was spinning because of the alcohol I'd consumed or from the desire that had finally burst through the lid I'd kept it contained under all night.

"Maggie Bennigan, I want to be with you. To feel every inch of your gorgeous body. But I'd rather you be able to remember all this in the morning."

"No, no, you don't understand." I had put my hands on either side of his face and pulled him even closer. "I want to, I really, really do. I swear I'll be able to remember in the morning. Even if I get Alzheimer's someday, I'll always remember this."

He had laughed. Then tenderly ran his fingertips through my hair. I closed my eyes; it felt so good, his gentle touch.

"I just don't want to fall in love with you." I had whispered.

"Why?" He had whispered back. "Am I so horrible?"

"No, you're a player. And too good-looking. And a Fed. I'm a cop. Never work out." I had murmured.

"If I was a player Maggie, wouldn't I be ripping your clothes off right now?"

I remember I had smiled. And then gave myself over to the sleep that was curling around me.

*   *   *   *

"Hey, you're up." Luke is standing in the doorway. Holding a cup of coffee. Wearing nothing but jean shorts and his killer smile.

"I must look like a train wreck." I pull the sheet up over my head.

"I think you're even prettier with dark smudges under your eyes and messed up hair." He sits next to me, pulls the sheet away.

"Coffee?" He hands me the cup. "I wasn't sure how you liked it so I put in two sugars and some cream."

"That's perfect. I like it sweet." I smile gratefully.

"How do you feel?"

"Like someone dropped me from the top of an apartment building and I landed on my head."

I sip the coffee. Then remembered.

"Oh God. What time is it?"

"Almost noon."

"Shit!" I hand him the cup, throwing back the covers. Thank God I am fully dressed.

"What's wrong?"

"It's Marty's birthday and I promised Becky I'd come to the cookout they're having for him; it starts at noon."

I grab my shoes, feeling as if my head is going to fall off my shoulders and roll under the bed.

"My keys? My cell phone?" I rush out of the room.

The living room is filled with overstuffed furniture in a green and blue check pattern. "Nice." I tell him over my shoulder.

"You mentioned that last night, right after you asked me if some guy named Todd decorated the place."

"Todd?" I ask while glancing at the coffee tables, searching for my stuff.

"Yeah, you said he was some gay guy you interviewed the other day."

"Oh, yes, Todd."

"Then I told you my sister helped me decorate and you wanted to see a picture of her."

"Here they are!" I grab them off the fireplace mantel and head for the door.

"Wait, I'll walk you to your car."

The pavement burns my feet and I stop to slip into my sandals, holding onto Luke's arm so I won't topple over.

"Do you think you'll be up for dinner tonight? A movie?" He asks as I climb into the Mustang. It smells like old french fries. I grip the hot steering wheel, trying not to gag in front of Luke. I can't believe he still wants to go out with me after the things I've said, after he has seen me looking my worst, and after getting a hefty whiff of my morning breath.

"I'd love to do dinner. I'll call you." I start the engine.

"You don't have my number." He reaches in, leans across me and grabs my cell phone.

A few minutes later, with the warm pressure of his lips still on my forehead, and his number added to my phone, I drive away, thinking Jake has Luke all wrong.

*   *   *   *

Becky is standing next to the grill, poking hot dogs and flipping hamburgers. She is wearing a chef's hat and a grin.

"It sounds like you're falling for him."

"No way." I'm holding a paper plate loaded with potato salad and baked beans, waiting for her to pile a hamburger onto a sesame bun. Some Tylenol, a cold shower, and I feel like I human being again. A starved human being.

"What you say is one thing. How you say it is another."

"What do you mean?"

"Well, you tell me about your night with him, how sweet he was and your face glows up and your eyes shine, and you have this little smile that makes me think of Susie when she talks about the new cute boy at school. And when you tell me that it's strictly "just for fun", you bite your lip and your shoulders sag. It's as if you're trying to believe what you are saying out loud, but inside, you're not so sure."

I sigh and glance around. Marty is talking to a group of his fire fighting buddies under a maple tree. Susie is splashing around the pool with a group of friends. This is what I think I so desperately want and yet, I had it. And it wasn't what I thought it would be. I still wanted to go out and have a good time; Ben wanted to snuggle on the couch and rent movies. I wanted to go to go to Flyers games and Eagles games; Ben wanted to invite his buddies over and watch them on TV.

After only a few years of marriage, I began to envy the single people I worked with. I started to go out once a week, getting so plastered, I'd have to spend the next day recuperating in bed. When I got divorced, Becky had assured me it wasn't that I didn't want to be married. I just didn't want to be married to Ben. "There IS someone out there for you, honey. Someone who will crave the same kind of excitement that you crave."

They say it's rare for people to find a great love. And I know 6 people who have it. Becky and Marty. Jake and Lucy. My mom and dad. That means my odds of winning the lottery are probably better than winning at love. At least I play the lottery once a week.

I'm in my own little world, not paying attention, when Becky adds a fat hamburger to my plate. I had been holding the flimsy paper disc with one hand. It slips from my grip and as it falls to the ground, the potato salad and baked beans somehow attach to my shorts.

"Shit," I moan.

"Oh God," Becky pushes the hat back on her head and laughs. "It looks like you threw up on yourself."

"Thanks." I'm so damn hungry too.

"Upstairs in my closet, there are some shorts on the shelves."

"Like I'll fit into them."

"Please. You're a whole five pounds heavier than I am. But if you feel uncomfortable wearing them, you can put on some sweatpants. I think they're under the shorts."

As I walk by the pool, kids start to laugh and point at me. Ha Ha Ha. I have a sudden urge for a shot of whiskey.

Becky's bedroom closet is immaculate. Her shoes are lined neatly. Her clothes are organized by season and colors. Short sleeve pastels, short sleeve primary colors. I stand on my tiptoes and dig through the shorts, trying to locate the sweat pants. I'm not even going to attempt to fit into anything else. She maybe only be five pounds lighter than I am, but she's also 4 inches taller.

My fingertips brush the familiar softness of sweat pants. I start to pull them slowly from the pile of shorts, trying not to unearth the tower of color. The sweats catch on something. I stretch my back as much as possible, and reach underneath. I can't see, but I can feel...

My hand knows this familiar object. The coolness of it, the smoothness. My arm retracts quickly as if it's a fishing line that has just been reeled in.

I sense someone behind me and turn; layer upon layer of heat attacks my cheeks.

"I'm looking for the other bathroom? Becky said there was one in her room?" It's a slightly tipsy guy that I recognize as one of Marty's friends.

"Right there," I nod toward the far side of the room.

"Quite a mess you got there." He looks at my shorts.

"Uh, yeah. I'm clumsy."

I want to yell at him, "Get the fuck outta here buddy."

But I give a small smile and close the door, shutting him out.

I reach back up and pull the object out.

It's a .38 service revolver. Even without any light in the closet, it gleams as I turn it over and over. It's not loaded. There's no clip in it. I hear a toilet flush and shove the gun back under the pile. I hurriedly step out of my shorts, pulling the gray sweat pants on.

"Maggie, you okay?" Becky knocks on the door.

Am I okay? Well, let's see. I just found a gun in my best friend's closet. My best friend who refuses to let her husband keep a gun in the house. It's 'too dangerous' with kids around. And 'most people who try to defend themselves with their own gun end up getting shot with it.' My best friend who won't let Susie spend the night at my house because I own guns. Who makes me leave my gun in the car when I come to visit.

"Yeah, I'm fine." I open the door.

"I just wanted to make sure." She watches Marty's friend walk out of the bedroom. "Didn't want him to see ya naked." She frowns, "Jesus, your face is beet red. Did something happen?"

"No." I step out of the closet. I feel as if my breath has been clipped right out of my chest with a pair of gardening shears.

"Just embarrassed I made such a mess."

She scrunches her face as if to say, "You embarrassed?" but instead says, "Jesus, don't worry about. I could think of worse things."

Yeah, I think as I follow her out, like finding the same caliber gun in your best friend's closet that was used in the murder of a pedophile.

It is not what a lawyer tells me I may do; but what humanity, reason, and justice tell me I ought to do.

—Edmund Burke

Whistle Stop park is located off of a somewhat busy street during the day but at night, traffic slows to a few cars every ten minutes or so. An abandoned gray factory with broken windows and cracked walls is separated from the park by obsolete train tracks. Across the street, hidden from view by large shrubs and trees, is the Remington Business Center where they manufacture office supplies.

I know the park well. During the day the broken swings, dented slides and splintered wooden train, have only each other for company. Parents have long since forsaken the Whistle Stop for newer playgrounds which boast castles, sand boxes, tire swings, and wooden mazes. The only people that visit the Whistle Stop are people who need a quiet, out of the way hiding spot. Teenagers. Lovers married to others. The occasional drug deal.

My car is parked across the street, at the Remington Business Center. I had called it earlier in the day and asked to speak to security. "I'm sorry, you must be mistaken, we don't have a security office here."

"Are you sure, Miss? I have a note here that says there's a problem with the wiring of the security cameras in the parking lot and my company is sending someone over to look at them."

The woman had cackled. "We don't even have air conditioning here. You must have the wrong company."

There are a few cars parked in the lot, the second shifters. Here is where things could get a little hairy. There was a possibility someone would see me entering or leav-

ing, though I didn't put much stock into it. The building is set far back from the parking lot. The chances of my getting caught are slim.

*As I wait behind the shelter of trees with the gun tucked in my waistband; I contemplate calling it off. I could walk back to my car; get on with my life. I have so much to lose. I know in my heart of hearts, I got away with T-Ray's murder. It was the perfect crime. If I walked away now, I walked away free. But then I remember my online chat with Mr. New York. How ballsy he was, how he wasted no time. For all he knew, I could have been a cop setting him up, and yet he was willing to risk it all for the glimpse of a 12 year olds privates. And what if I **had** been a 12 year old? What if he was planning on doing more than looking?*

Headlights cut a yellow line through the park as they enter. I hedge forward. I am just behind the entrance. It is a Lexus; dark in color. New York license plate.

The car slowly inches along until it comes to the edge of the parking lot, facing the forlorn playground equipment. The headlights dim.

I back out of the trees until I'm on the road. Any doubt I had is pushed out of my mind as my body takes over and carries me along. I'm dressed in black shorts, a long sleeved black t-shirt, running shoes. I start to jog a few paces, and the blacktop soon turns into gravel under my feet.

"Dempsey, here boy…Dempsey…" I call out, my voice filling the dusty air. I continue to jog, holding a leash in my sweaty hands. "Dempsey, c'mon you mutt." I slow down as I approach the parked car. I can make out the balding head of a man behind the wheel. He turns to look at me. His face is long, lean. The face of a serious businessman. A trader on Wall Street? A lawyer?

I wave the leash in the air.

The window makes a hissing sound as it descends.

"I'm looking for my dog; she's a German Shepard. You haven't seen her, have you?"

"Sorry. Get away from you, did she?"

"She did. I should know better than to let her off the leash." I shake my head. "You a Yankee's fan?" I fold myself over, placing my hands on my knees so I can look in his eyes.

The color from his face drains quickly and he looks over his shoulder, behind me, as if a cop car is gonna drive through the bushes. It's the confirmation I need.

"I saw your license plate, you're from New York?"

He nods. Presses the button and the window begins to climb upward.

Shit.

"My dad played for the Yankees." I throw the words out; watch them land.

The window stops.

"God, don't tell him this, but I carry a baseball around for my dog to fetch. Its got his autograph on it. You'll freak out when you see who he is." I reach into my waistband, never taking my eye off him. He glances behind me again.

As quick as his eyes dart from the bushes and back to me, the gun is out, glinting in the moonlight. I pull the trigger before his mind is able to comprehend what is about to happen.

Pop. A flash of light.

His body slumps to the side. I step forward, reach into the car and place the barrel directly against his forehead. Pull the trigger again. I cannot take the risk that the first bullet did not do its job.

Satisfied, I take a handkerchief out of my pocket and wrap it around the gun before tucking it into my shorts. The barrel is hot. I don't want to burn my skin.

I wrap the leash around my hand and begin the jog back to my car.

Detective Bennigan
August 4, Sunday. Afternoon

Here is where I know I should ask Becky about the gun. If I do not ask her now, I risk carrying the information around with me like a mosquito I can't shake. Buzzing in my ear and biting me; an irritating reminder of what I know, what it could mean.

As we walk down the steps, her daughter and a pigtailed friend rush past us, droplets of water jumping from their skin to ours.

"In or out, Susan. And make sure you dry off before coming into the house." Becky calls after the giggling kids. She rolls her eyes at me. "This is going to be a long day."

And I think, this is my chance, pull her aside. Take her in the family room and ask her about it. It will be a simple explanation, something that will make me laugh. Instead, I follow her through the kitchen, back out to the bright sunlight.

Okay, maybe if I eat something. Maybe once I have something of substance in my belly besides Tylenol and water. But as I pick up another plate, I find I'm not so hungry.

Marty has taken Becky's place at the grill. She stands at the edge of the pool, telling the kids it's time to come out and get something to eat. They groan and protest and she picks up some pool toys that are lying on the concrete and wings them playfully into the water.

When I was going through my divorce and felt like the whole world was closing in on me, I knew that by picking up the phone and calling her, I would be smiling within minutes. To think that Becky was in anyway involved in the murder of T-Ray Austin is absurd.

I pick a potato chip from a bowl and place it on my tongue, allowing it to dissolve. Becky stands by the pool steps, doling out towels to the kids as they climb the silver ladder. I realize I have to ask her about the gun. If I wait, she will wonder why I didn't confront her when I found it. She'll be able to read the doubt that I harbored and this will shake the foundation of our friendship. Above all else, Becky regales honesty and communication.

I start to walk toward her when Marty reaches out and lightly grabs my arm.

"Your cell phone is ringing, Maggie." He tips his head toward the picnic table, where my cell phone is glinting in the afternoon light.

"Oh, thanks." The ring is shrill and angry, like a hungry newborn wondering why her mother has disappeared.

I flip it open, waving my arm, trying to catch Becky's attention.

"Hey, Maggie. It's Tom. Is your dog licking your toes?"

A feeling of dread tackles me and I sink onto the bench. "No, I'm at a party. So this better be good."

"It is. Respond to the Whistle Stop Park. Guy shot in the head. Chet and Stu initially got the case, but they think you and Nate should be there."

"Shit." I stand up, grab my purse. "Why do they want us there?"

"I don't know for sure. But they ran the dead guy's name through NCIC and he came up as a registered sex offender."

"Fuck." I say out loud and several partygoers, including kids, snap their heads back and look at me. "Sorry." I apologize and head over to Becky, who is rounding the last two kids out of the pool.

"I'll be there in ten minutes." I tell Tom before snapping the phone shut.

"I have to go. There's been another homicide," I whisper to her. "I'm so sorry."

"For what? You've got the most exciting job imaginable. Just call when you get a chance and let me know what's going on."

"Sure." I push open the gate. "Beck?"

"Yeah?" She shields her eyes with her hand and squints against the sun.

I lose my nerve. "Sorry I made such a mess."

She cocks her head to the side, something flashes across her eyes...a question, an answer, a doubt?

"Don't worry about it. I guess your dinner with Luke is off?"

Oh God. I forgot.

"I guess so." I kick the ground with my foot. Which isn't too smart as I'm wearing sandals. I end up yelping in pain. "God, I hate my job."

"Margaret Lousie Bennigan. You liar. You love your job." Becky grins, making things right, easing the pain throbbing in my big toe.

"You're right. I do love my job. Otherwise I wouldn't put up with missed parties and dates, not being able to spend more time with Zoey..." I give her a hug; feel the warmth of her hair against my cheek. This is my best friend. My sister in spirit. Becky Carpenter is not a killer. I laugh out loud at the absurdity of it.

"That's what I like to hear." She kisses my cheek and pushes me out into the world.

*   *   *   *

Nate's Jeep is pulling into the park when I arrive.

"What are you doing here?" I ask him as I crawl out of the car.

"They called me off suspension. Said they think this is related to T-Ray. I should finish what I've started."

I squeeze his arm. "Glad to have you back. How do you feel?"

"Like you look."

I purse my lips and narrow my eyes. "Thanks."

A band of sweat has formed around my waist and under my breasts. Somewhere a frog is croaking, probably literally. The smell of alcohol drifts my way.

I steal a sidelong glance at Nate. He is unshaven, his hair tousled as if he's just climbed out of bed. Jake meets us mid stride before I can say anything to Nate.

"Jesus, Nate, tuck in your shirt." Jake motions with his head, "Reporters are staked out on the other side of the park."

I lift my eyes and see them crowded together, pressed against the yellow police tape line strung in, out, and around a line of trees that shade the park.

"Damn, they're fast." Nate breathes and it's unmistakable now, the smell of malt and yeast.

I brace myself for Jake's nuclear explosion but all he does is step back and flips open his notepad. "Roger Buckley. 45. From New York City. Was arrested in 1996 for molestation. Served 45 days. Five years probation. Convicted of molesting his girlfriends 10 year old son." He snaps the gum in his mouth. "A jogger called 911 around 2pm and reported a man passed out in a car. Ambulance arrived and found he was shot in the head. Twice. So far, no eyewitnesses. Medical examiner is enroute. Guy looks like he's been here for a while. Rigamortis has set in."

Jake tucks the notebook back in the pocket of his shorts. "Maggie, the jogger is sitting on the park bench; do you want to talk to her?"

"C'mon Jake, you owe me. Why don't you talk to her?" I plead.

I need to pull Nate aside and make sure what I'm smelling is the residual left-over from our night at the Tex Mex.

Jake shakes his head and sighs, "When I'm at home, I get grief. I come to work, and I get grief. My wife is pregnant. What's your excuse?"

"I haven't had a day off in ages. I was enjoying myself at a party when this came in and the last person I interviewed who found a dead body gave me his life story and I'm really not in the mood to listen to a half hour of bullshit before I get the answers to the questions I need."

"You know what Maggie, your problem is that you're too nice to people. You let them go on and on about their life story. You gotta cut them off and get right to the subject at hand."

"Okay, then you go talk to her and show me how it's done." I cross my arms. A challenge. Jake can't refuse one.

"Fine." He takes off his sunglasses, slides them in his pocket and Nate and I watch him walk away.

Once he's out of hearing range, I grab Nate and pull him close.

"You reek of alcohol. What the fuck is going on?"

"Jesus, Maggie, I thought I was suspended. The guys and I were at home putting a few back when the call came in."

"Well, you should have said you couldn't come in."

"Oh, right. Tell the Chief, who I'm already in the doghouse with, that I had a few beers and couldn't make it in? C'mon Maggie, I'm already in deep shit."

"That's right. You're already in deep shit and what's gonna happen if someone figures out you've been drinking?" I dig inside my purse, searching for a stray mint or piece of gum. A single Altoid, that may or may not have been spit out by Zoey, clings to the bottom.

"Here," I press it into his hand. "Stay away from Jake, talk as little as possible."

He turns the white disk over in his hand.

"Put it in your mouth," I hiss, stepping in front of him to shield him from the eyes of the reporters.

"I think this has been sucked on before Maggie."

"Jesus, Nate. Just put it in your fucking mouth."

Jake is shaking hands with the jogger, closing his notebook, heading our way.

Nate drops the mint in his mouth, winks at me, then ambles over to the Lexus; his stride as confident as John Wayne's. The fingerprint kit is tucked under his left arm.

"Well?" I ask Jake who arrives by my side with a smug grin on his face.

"Out for a jog. Noticed the car. Noticed a guy slumped over and wasn't sure if he passed out or was sleeping something off. Calls 911 and waits for the ambulance. That's it."

"Good for you. From now on, you can handle the interviews, you're so good at it."

"God, you're cranky. I guess you didn't get laid last night, after all." Jake glides the pen over the top of his ear.

"I wouldn't tell you if I did." Fatigue glides over my bones and it takes energy for my brain to make a sentence. "Any thoughts as to the weapon that was used?"

Jake shrugs. "Looks like it could be a .38. Same as T-Ray."

Across the park, the reporters are shouting questions at the uniforms who are still busy combing the park for clues.

"Looks like we've got us a serial killer, eh?" I exhale.

"You know, you should be a detective."

"Funny. You're funny." I start to head for the car. Jake jumps in front of me.

"You notice anything about Nate?"

"Like what?" I keep my head down.

"Smells like he's been drinking."

"Nah." I look up, meet Jake's dark quizzical eyes. "We had a lot to drink last night. He just rolled out of bed when he got the call. Didn't shower." I shrug. "He didn't want to take the time out to get cleaned up. Didn't want to arrive late since he got the go ahead to come back."

Jake looks at me like my father did when I was 16 and came home ten minutes after my curfew. My dad *wanted* to believe the movie started late. He *didn't* want to think his daughter was sitting in a parked car making out with her boyfriend.

"Tell him to take the extra five minutes to shower and brush his teeth."

"Will do, Captain." I salute.

As we join the cluster of people circling around the crime scene, I make a checklist of things in my mind. Call Luke. Cancel plans. Keep Jake away from Nate. Confront Becky about gun? Get some damn food.

A man who has nothing for which he is willing to fight, nothing which is more important than his own personal safety, is a miserable creature and has no chance of being free unless made and kept so by the exertions of better men than himself."

—John Stuart Mill

What I've found interesting in reading the paper is the Letters to the Editor section. It amazes me that once a week there is a new story about a kid getting molested and yet, the only stories that incite people enough that they put pen in hand, are the stories about abused dogs. Or the articles about the proposed widening of a major highway, or the fight between the volunteer fire company and the township that wants to hire paid firefighters to phase out the volunteers. Very rarely are readers concerned with the fact that children are being targeted by sick men. I love animals…but why is it that people are more concerned with the plight of a family pet than the rape of an innocent child?

On Monday, after the story broke about the murder of T-Ray and the murder of Roger Buckley, my faith in humans was somewhat restored; the paper was flooded with letters, and not one mentioned dogs or cats.

Dear Editor:

Are the murders of two convicted pedophiles linked? Who cares? Is there a serial killer on the loose? Who cares? As long as pedophiles are the target, I say it's about time someone did something about these sickos. I know if someone harmed my kids, I'd do the very same thing.

Dear Editor,
*   Who could blame this man you have labeled the 'Pedophile Predator'? Frankly, I think of this guy as Superman. What kind of system keeps spewing out these social degenerates? Justice has not been served if a convicted molester does time, is released back into society and continues to stalk children. Perhaps we have developed a society which is too lenient on criminals. Someone has identified the problem and is seeking to correct it. I'd personally post bail for the Pedophile Predator...*

Dear Editor:
*   So it has come to this? Molesters afraid they might have to pay a price for destructing our most precious commodity, children. Maybe they will think twice before touching another child.*

Dear Editor,
*   While I do not in anyway condone children being harmed, I do not agree with the murder of pedophiles. If everyone took justice into their hands, the population would dwindle to nothing. This killer may think he is righting the wrongs done to children, but two wrongs do not make a right. He needs to be caught and pay for his crimes.*

Dear Editor,
*   I have one word to say about the Pedophile Predator: Hero.*

I smile at this last letter. I have not set out to be a hero. I know what I do is wrong. But wrong only because our society makes it so. In Sociology, I learned the definition of normal is set by what the majority of a group of people felt is normal. If the popular consensus of a society decided that wearing black socks meant that you were an evil person, most people would throw out their black socks and regard those who went against the grain as wicked.
*   Our society has been set up to protect. Our society has been devised so that those who commit crimes have a second, third, fourth, and a forever chance to begin again.*

And for the most part, I agree that those who have stumbled in their ways should be given a fresh slate. Pay for their wrongs and then right themselves.

But when it comes to pedophiles…it has been proven time and time again, these perverts cannot stop their desire for young flesh. And in the interest of protecting the perverts, in the interest of making sure that they get their "day in court" that their rights have not been compromised in anyway, we as a society go far and above the call of duty.

Perhaps I am the wakeup call we so desperately need. That is my hope, my intention. If enough people band together, if enough people can open their eyes and see this as I see it, maybe the laws will change. Maybe not. But perhaps the next time a pedophile is swept away in his desire for the taste of innocent flesh, he will wonder if the consequences are worth the actions.

Detective Bennigan
August 6, Tuesday. Morning

A cup of lukewarm stale coffee sits on the bench waiting for me as I shove my purse into my locker. Dog-tired wouldn't be the proper word for what sits in my bones and begs me to lie somewhere, anywhere, even on the concrete floor that squeaks under my shoes.

Jake had grabbed me before I ducked into the women's locker room. His face not only tired, but anger left red marks on his cheeks. "Chief wants to see us in ten minutes. I think he's calling in the FBI."

"What?" The sleeplessness that clung to me was chased away by a shot of adrenaline.

"The murder on Sunday crossed state lines. We might be dealing with a serial killer. Two protocols for calling in the Feds."

The air-conditioning was still on the lam, and the dimly lit hallway smelled like rotting vegetables.

"Have you talked to Luke? Has he said anything about it?" Jake wanted to know.

"The only time I talked to Luke was when I called to tell him I couldn't make it to dinner on Sunday night. Remember? You were sitting next to me in the car rolling your eyes."

I check my watch and sit on the bench. I have a few minutes before I have to show my face in the conference room. We have nothing to go on. No clues, no fibers, no fingerprints, no eyewitnesses. Zilch. I haven't had a chance to call Becky.

Late Sunday night I picked up Zoey from Ben's house and then got her up at the crack of dawn to get her to daycare. I hate rousing her from her sleep, her sweet face lost in a smile, encompassed in a good dream. Early Monday evening, when I had rescued her from daycare, only two children remained. I tried to cheer myself with the thought that at least she wasn't the last to go. When we get home, I tried to focus on coloring, bathing, and reading her "Good Night Moon" but my thoughts kept drifting back to the murders, back to the gun in Becky's house, back to the taste of Luke's mouth on mine. And then I was up again at the crack of dawn this morning to repeat the whole process.

"Yo, Maggie." There is rap on the locker room door. "Chief's waiting in the conference room."

I open the door to find Nate on the other side. He is freshly shaven, back to his old self. We walk up a flight of stairs. Nate holds a box of doughnuts and their sweet scent makes my stomach launch into a series of belly flops.

"You get crème filled ones?" I ask.

"Of course. I kept one hidden in my locker just in case they get raided and you don't get one."

"Thata boy." I pat him on the back.

As soon as we enter the conference room, I'm assaulted by a variety of smells that loiter in the oppressive air; aftershave, deodorant, sweaty armpits, coffee, and minty mouthwash.

I slide into a seat next to Jake, and Nate slips next to me, our backs to the door. Chief Hightower is standing at the head of the table. His bald head is dotted with beads of perspiration that he continuously mops with a gray handkerchief.

Nate pushes the pink-stripped doughnut box to the center of table. As hands reach out to attack it, there is a sudden shift in the air and the hands withdraw. I look across the table at the faces of my comrades. They are eyeing the door.

Jake and I look over our shoulder at the same time. My heart catches and lights with excitement and dread.

Luke enters first, wearing a blue suit, his eyes shining as they meet mine. He is followed by a man shaped like a marshmallow, with a bulbous red nose and what appears to be a grape jelly stain on his tie.

Chief Hightower waves to them, signals them to sit in the chairs next to him that everyone has steered clear of.

Jake exhales slowly, his hot breath lands on my folded hands.

The doughnut box remains untouched. The room has stilled. The feds and cops have a hate hate relationship. To cops, the feds are the kids in high school who got the good grades because they brown-nosed the teachers. The guys who drove to high school in shiny red sports cars while the rest of us walked, or worse, rode the bus.

We all know why they are here. Protocol. We have the flu, and they are chicken soup and herbal tea. We don't have the stomach for it, but we know we must swallow it because it's what the doctor ordered.

Chief Hightower clears his throat. "Good morning everyone. I'm not going to waste any time with pleasantries this morning. As you guys know, the murder of T-Ray Austin and Roger Buckley have caused quite an uproar in the community." His gaze flickers over us, somehow takes us in individually as well as a whole.

"Ballistics pinpoint the murder weapon to a .38 service revolver. The victims have histories as sex offenders. That's all we know right now. Due to the fact we may be working with a serial killer, and that Mr. Buckley was from New York, we've asked the FBI to join in the investigation."

There is a small titter among the group that is immediately silenced by the daggers Hightower unleashes.

"Most of you are familiar with Luke Foreman. He will work with Jake and Maggie, who will continue to head the investigation. Luke is joined by Agent Thomas Groves."

Bulbous nose gives us a curt nod. Hightower continues, "The media is having a field day with this. No one is to speak to them. I'll meet with Jake and Maggie each day at 5pm and we'll decide from there what to say to the media, if anything. In the event of another murder, I'm to be notified ASAP." Hightower breaks for another sip of water. I steal a glance at Luke, who is staring at a yellow legal pad in front of him. My mouth is dry and I have no choice but to take a drink of coffee that has grown cold and bitter.

"Look. I know several of you, most of you, think these guys deserved to be murdered. I'm not asking you to feel any sort of sympathy for them, but I am asking that you make sure you do everything by the book. I don't want to hear that my guys were saying Austin and Buckley got what they had coming. The fact is, two men were murdered and it's our job to find out who did it and hand them over to the D.A.. If anyone has doubts about their ability to do this job, and do it right, see me in private and I'll remove you from this case. Any questions?"

Silence. Nate's leg is bouncing under the table, I put my hand on his knee, squeeze gently.

"Okay, why don't the rest of you leave, and Jake and Maggie…" Hightower nods in our direction, "you guys stay behind and bring Agents Foreman and Groves up to speed on the investigation."

I excuse myself, saying I have to use the bathroom but promise I'll be right back. I escape out into the hall. The truth is, I need to splash some cool water on my face and try to come up with a quick game plan as to how I'm going to handle Luke's presence.

The guys are walking down the steps, and I catch a few words being muttered under their breath. "Bullshit." "Assholes" "Fucking crap".

I turn down the hallway that leads to the locker rooms. Nate is pressed against the wall, a cigarette dangling from his mouth.

"Can't you light up outside? This place is a damn tomb as it is. We don't need your cigarette smoking polluting it more."

He shrugs.

"I thought you were so concerned about keeping your job?" I take the butt out of his mouth, intending to crush it under my shoe. I have a change of heart and take a quick drag.

"What's wrong?" I exhale.

He shrugs.

"Are you pissed the FBI got called in?"

He shakes his head.

I don't have time to play games with him. "Whatever, Nate." I hand him back the cigarette. "It's your funeral."

I push open the door to the woman's locker room and head to the sink. The water is cool against my clammy skin. As I look in the mirror, Nate's face appears behind me.

"Jesus." I grab the side of the sink. "Don't fucking sneak up on me like that."

"Maggie." He gives me his country singer eyes.

I wait.

"When I was nine, I hung out with this kid, Lenny. He had the best bike and cool electronic toys. His mom was always baking cakes and cookies and feeding us every ten minutes. One summer night, me and Lenny were sleeping in a tent in the backyard." Nate leans against a locker, staring at the floor as if the story he is telling me is being projected on the concrete. I rest against the sink, feeling the chill of the porcelain bite into my back.

"I have this dream that a snake is wrapping around my dick. It feels so real...you know how like you have a dream that you're peeing and you wake up and realize you've wet the bed?" His eyes shift and meet mine.

I nod. Realize I'm holding my breath. He looks back at the floor and I look too. I can see the tent; I can see Nate with gangly arms, hair bleached from spending his days out in the sun racing bikes, playing cops and robbers, fishing.

"I wake up, thinking maybe a snake has crawled in my shorts. I mean, we were in the backyard and all."

A blast of cold air shakes itself out of the vent above us.

"I open my eyes and there he is; Lenny's dad. With his hand around my dick. He pulls it away, acting like it was never there. He says he came out to let me know that Lenny got scared and went in the house to sleep in his room."

My body shudders. "What did you do? What did you say?"

"Jesus, Maggie. I was nine. I had no idea what to do. I spent the rest of the night sitting up, waiting for the sun to rise. As soon as it did, I biked two miles home. Never mentioned it to anyone. Thought maybe it was just a dream, though I knew it wasn't."

"What about Lenny?"

Nate shrugs. "What about him? I stopped hanging around with him, he never asked why. Boys do that. It's no big deal." He reaches up, twists his hand in the draft of chilled air. "'Bout time they fixed it. Give it a few days, it'll choke and we'll be swimming in our sweat again."

I turn the faucet on and watch as the water runs over my hands. "I'm sorry…"

He waves my words away. "Hey, you know, most kids have a lot worse happen to them. I just remember that at nine years old, the fact a grown man was digging in my shorts fucked my head up for about a year. Actually, a lot longer than that."

"These murders…they bring it back?" My skin is covered in goose pimples. I hug my arms across my chest.

"Maggie, if I got fucked up over some guy touching me, I can't even imagine what kids who have been truly violated must feel. Austin and Buckley, they got what they had coming."

"Maybe you should ask to be removed from the case?"

Nate grimaces like I've just kicked him in the balls. "And what reason would I give? I don't want people knowing my business. I don't want my family whispering about it. Hell, my father wouldn't even believe it. He'd just think I was trying to make up some reason to excuse my recklessness."

I nod. He is right. Chief Hightower and his brother are football loving, beer drinking, keep all emotion tucked at the bottom of the tackle box, sort of men.

"Anything I can do…"

"Just don't tell anyone." He shoves his hands deep in his pockets. "I only wanted you to know because I don't want you to think I'm the fuck up everyone else thinks I am."

I smile and finally reach out to him, careful not to pull him too close. Heat rolls off his body and warms me. "Nate, you are the little brother I never had."

"Damn, you think of me as your brother? Does this mean I'll never get you in the sack?"

"No way," I laugh, the tension in the room is sucked into the sink, swirls down the drain. "I might be horny, but I'm not that horny."

I think the purpose of life is to be useful, to be responsible, to be honorable, to be compassionate. It is, after all, to matter: to count, to stand for something, to have made some difference that you lived at all.

—Leo C. Rosten

I have been following my next victim, Charles Wentworth, for a few days.

He lives alone in a three-story brick apartment building in one of the better sections of North Twilight. There is a shopping center across the street. A Barnes and Noble, Target and TGIF restaurant that draws smart, savvy and hungry shoppers.

Mr. Wentworth has been spending hours each day tucked in an overstuffed pea green chair at Barnes and Noble, perusing magazines and travel books. I've walked by him on several occasions but he is so ensconced in his reading, or perhaps in his mind, wondering about what his future holds, that he has not noticed me.

He worked at Dillion's Hardware store as a sales rep before his arrest for attempting to molest the 12-year-old boy at the mall parking lot. Somehow, he came up with the ten thousand dollars that was set as his bail. When the paper reported he made bail and was released until his trial date, I knew what I had to do.

I wasn't sure exactly when an opportunity would present itself and only had a few hours a day in which to follow my mark.

The news has been reporting today is the hottest day of the year; a group of kids almost succeeded in frying an egg on the sidewalk. I wondered what an almost fried egg looked like.

Charles Wentworth leaves Barnes and Noble and walks across the street to his apartment building.

Very few cars are parked in the lot.

I climb out of my rental car aware of a loud hum vibrating through the humidity; it is the air-conditioning units, working overtime.

The Barnes and Noble bag clutched under my arm holds the latest People magazine and my gun.

The carpet on the stairs is worn, rust colored. Someone has been frying onions.

Apartment C-4, second floor.

In the back of my mind, a hesitation. Wentworth has lost his job. He is going to stand trial in a few weeks. Life as he has known it has been destroyed.

I pull open the door that has a gold C stamped on the window.

The hesitation passes quickly as I remind myself why I'm here. Wentworth did prison time for molestation and yet he didn't learn his lesson the first time. If he's convicted, what will happen when he's released after another five years? The same damn thing, perhaps even worse. He could have reformed himself. He didn't. And who knows how many kids he may have come into contact with before the twelve year old. How many children are carrying around a scar on their soul that bears the name Wentworth?

There are four doors on this floor; I stop and quickly listen at each one.

Silence.

I have half an hour before my absence will be noticed.

With my elbow, I gently knock against C-4.

All I can hear is the hum of the air conditioner. A peephole peers at me. I try to keep my face open, friendly.

A deadbolt is released. The door opens and there he stands. A smile on his chapped lips.

"Yes?"

"I think you forgot this?" I raise the Barnes and Noble bag a bit.

"Oh, no. You must be mistaken...I..."His voice trails as I reach into the bag.

Pull out the gun.

He opens his mouth to...yell? Protest? I'll never know as the bullet pierces his skull. The shot is dead center.

I am about to turn when a gasp grabs my legs.

I step inside the room, my eyes wild, my heart hammering and ranting like a buck caught in a hunter's scope.

An older woman, hair wrapped in a white towel and wearing a black robe that engulfs her small frame, stands frozen behind a leather couch.

I thought Wentworth lived alone; I was almost sure of it. I'd followed him for three days and hadn't seen a woman, man, child, dog; nothing. He was the only person who emerged and entered the apartment. "Oh God." Her words are a whisper, a plea. Her hands gather round the material at the neck of the robe.

I have no choice.

I have no choice.

I raise the gun. I want to turn away from her, I don't want to meet her eyes, but I have to make this shot count.

She falls to the carpet; her thin body barely makes a sound as it lands.

What The Fuck.

I have no choice. A .38 at a distance is not enough to assure a kill.

Her eyes are closed; her hands have fallen away from the robe and are now pressed together, as if she is praying.

Another shot against her temple.

The bagel I'd had for lunch lurches into my throat. I cannot stop it from advancing.

I'm still holding the Barnes and Noble bag. I retch inside it. Even when my stomach is emptied, hollow, I still heave.

I make my way to the door, my body still violently quaking.

Detective Bennigan
August 9, Friday. Afternoon

"Where are your cigarettes?" Jake opens the glove compartment, pushing napkins, receipts, and crayons out of the way.

"What are you doing?" I take my hand off the steering wheel and push his arm away.

"I know you're smoking again. I've seen you light up in the car after work. And you're chewing gum all the time and you practically douse your body in that vanilla spray you always wear."

I hate smelling like an ashtray. So I try to compensate.

"*You* want one of my cigarettes?"

Jake glances in the rearview mirror. "Is he right behind us?"

I sigh. "Yes, Luke is following us."

"Why did you have to invite him to Happy Hour? Can't we have a break from his Holy Presence? Isn't enough I have to work next to him day and night while you two are making goo goo eyes at each other."

"We aren't making goo goo eyes." I pull a pack of cigarettes out from under the seat and wave it in the air. "Is this because you're stressed about Lucy being overdue or because we have no leads or because Luke is working with us?"

"Yes." He grabs the pack and presses the car lighter.

My cell phone vibrates in my pocket.

"That better not be another dead pedophile on the phone." Jake puts a cigarette in his mouth. I wish I had a camera.

I recognize the number.

"It's Becky. Shhh," I warn him. "Hey Beck," I keep my voice light.

"I know you've been busy and all, but Christ, a phone call takes five minutes. I've missed you."

"I'm sorry, Becky." I grab the cigarettes from Jake and shake one out. "Hey, we're two minutes away from happy hour at the Tex Mex, can you make it?"

"As a matter of fact, I just dropped off Susie at my parents' house for the weekend. Marty is working."

"Great. I'll save you a spot."

"You know the jury is deliberating on the Westerfield trial, right?"

I smile at Jake; he is trying not to choke on the smoke as he inhales.

"No, honey. We've been so tied up…haven't had time to breathe let alone watch any TV or read any papers."

"If you called me once in awhile, I could keep you informed."

After we hang up, I take a long drag.

"Becky's coming?" Jake coughs.

"Yeah," I tap rhythmically on the steering wheel. The image of the gun in the closet has been hovering around my mind like a ghost over a grave.

"Could you ever imagine Becky killing anyone?" I ask.

Jake presses a button and the window zips down, letting hot air in and smoky air out.

"What? Becky? Why, is Marty having an affair or something?"

"Oh God, no." I laugh at the thought. "Just thinking, you know, about Austin and Buckley. How a parent who is normally docile and good could go berserk if they found out someone molested their kid."

Jake shakes his head. "I could see you killing someone if they hurt Zoey before I could see Becky killing someone. But I suppose anything is possible." He looks out the window, staring at the stores as they flash by. Randy's Pizza (too saucy), Second Hand Buy's (place smells like mothballs and dust), Sweet Tooth (still has penny candy). "Sometimes you think you know someone, you don't. We all have a side to us that we like to keep hidden."

I pull into the parking lot of the Tex Mex. "You have a side to you, Jake, that I don't know about?"

He grins, lifts his cigarette in the air. "Did you ever see the day when I'd be chomping on a butt?"

I laugh and unfold myself from the car. "Can't say I ever really thought about it."

Jake sighs loudly as Luke pulls in the lot.

"I'll go get us some seats," he leaps out of the car and sprints to the backdoor.

"Hey," Luke smiles at me as he slams his car door.

"Hey yourself," I soften.

He stands close to me, his body blocking the sun. I've come to know him better this past week: He likes oil on his ham hoagies and prefers Pepsi to Coke. When he disagrees with something, he'll tent his fingers and tap them together before speaking, choosing his words carefully, his voice becoming husky yet silky, enticing everyone to share his viewpoint. The way his eyes crinkle when he's deep in thought. I've come to sense when his eyes are following me, feeling their warmth on my legs, chest, shoulders, until they reach my gaze, at which point we share a smile, a secret desire.

The nights after work when he has called, I've had to apologize that I couldn't talk, I had to spend time with Zoey. I'd promise that after she was asleep, I'd call him. But after crawling into bed with Zoey to read her to sleep, I'd wake up with the morning, the sun spilling on the books that had fallen to the floor during the night.

Luke was understanding and patient. The longing I felt for him twisted around my heart so ferociously, at times it squeezed the blood right out of the chambers and left me feeling dizzy and breathless. And this made me very, very, afraid.

"Zoey's at her dad's house tonight?" Luke tucks a stray strand of hair behind my ear.

"All weekend." The skin on my ear tingles at his touch.

"Maybe we could replay last Saturday, with a little less alcohol?" His slow, easy smile.

I want to scream at the top of my lungs, yes, Yes, YES. Instead, I tell him;

"I don't know. The case and all. Is it a good idea? Mixing love with business?"

"I thought you said you weren't going to fall in love with me?"

My heart plunges off the high dive into an empty pool. Thud. Crack.

"I said that?"

"Last week, at my house? You were drunk." His voice is soft, letting me know he is not making fun of me, he is not teasing me. "You said something to the effect you only wanted to sleep with me, not fall in love with me because you thought I was a player."

"Oh, well." I throw my shoulders back, scoop up my heart. "Yeah, I still think you're a player."

A car pulls in behind us, so close I can feel the heat of the engine on my legs. I look over my shoulder, ready to bawl out the driver.

Becky sticks her tongue out at me.

"Maggie," Luke puts a finger on my chin and gently moves my head so that I'm looking at him. "I would never get involved with someone I was working with unless I was sure it was the right thing to do."

Becky bounces over to me and flings her arms around me, smiling up at Luke. "Nice to see you FBI guy."

"That's Special Agent Foreman, to you," he winks. "I'll go keep Jake company."

My heart has taken another dive. As I watch him walk away, my insides shimmer like the heat on the black top.

"You never mentioned he was coming."

"He's working the case with us." I catch my breath, focus on her.

She's cut her hair a few inches. Her face is not as tan. It's been less than a week since I've seen her, and yet it seems like years.

"You have to fill me in on everything. The paper makes it sound like you guys have nothing to go on."

It's now or never.

"Beck, before we go in? There's something I have to ask you."

"Okay." She frowns at the seriousness of my voice.

"At the party, Sunday? When I was getting those sweat pants out of the closet?" I watch her face carefully, trying to gauge her expression. Does she know what I'm going to say? Is her mind churning for an explanation to the question I'm going to pose?

She nods, waiting for me to go on.

The words rush out, "Under that pile of shorts, I found a gun."

Her eyes are empty. Blank. Then she throws back her blonde hair and laughs. "That's funny. A gun in my closet. Have you been drinking already?"

I don't move; don't breathe. For the first time since discovering it, it dawns on me that the gun could belong to Marty. But why would he be foolish enough to hide it under his wife's clothes?

She stops laughing when she realizes I'm not smiling.

"Maggie. You've got to be mistaken. You know how I feel about guns."

"I wouldn't mistake finding a .38 service revolver in your closet."

Becky shakes her head, "No, no. That's crazy. There would never be a gun in my house. Marty knows how I feel about it. All his friends know how I feel. Everyone who knows me, who knows us." Her eyes float around the parking lot, searching for an answer. "Why didn't you ask me about it then? Why didn't you show it to me? I was standing in that closet with you."

"I…You know…the gun used in the murders…Well, I was shocked. I didn't know how…"

Her hands fly to her hips as realization slaps her across the face, leaving a pink mark in its wake.

"Of course, you guys know what kind of gun was used in the murders. You thought I could have something to do with it?" She laughs coldly. "God, that's a stretch Maggie, even for you. Jesus, I'm your best friend. You've known me all your life. You think I could be remotely involved in something like that?" There is a shift in her eyes as sadness replaces her anger. She turns on her heel and walks to her car. I trail behind.

"Becky, wait, I…I just didn't know what to do; what to say."

She opens the car door, turns around and her voice is calm, "You could have shown the gun to me and asked me what it was doing in my closet."

As the engine revs, I hear my name being called.

Jake and Luke are walking toward me. Becky backs the car out and drives away without a goodbye, a wave, not even a glance.

"Double homicide at the Royal Town Apartments." Jake watches Becky's car as it pulls out into the street.

"Double? But that's not our killer's M.O." I remind him.

"Guy that got it is Charles Wentworth, name ring a bell?"

I want to drop to the ground and beat my legs and arms against the blacktop, even if it is one hundred and ten degrees. Instead I unlock the car doors. "Let's go."

*   *   *   *

I'm in the bedroom of the Wentworth apartment, going through the suitcase on the bed. It belongs to the dead woman, Veronica Brooding. Charles Wentworth's older sister, who according to airplane tickets on the dresser, had arrived on the red eye flight last night from Denver.

"Wow, she obviously had some bucks." With gloved hands, I rifle through the clothes. "All these labels are Donna Karan, and look," I hold a pair of dainty blue heels with diamond studded flowers attached to the straps, "Jimmy Choo shoes"

"God Bless you." Jake said absentmindedly, shuffling through papers on a desk.

I sigh. "I didn't sneeze, Jake. I said, these are Jimmy Choo shoes."

He looks up, "Who's Jimmy Choo?"

"Forget it." I put the shoes back gently. I'd have to skip a mortgage payment to afford a pair of Jimmy's shoes.

"Hey guys." Nate appears in the doorway. A dazzling beauty of a woman with flowing red hair and creamy white legs crawling out of tight denim shorts is directly behind him.

"What's the scoop?" Nate is sporting a baseball cap and a blue muscle shirt.

"Who's that?" Jake growls like a lion protecting his den.

"This is my date, Nicole. Nicole, Jake and Maggie." He introduces us as if we are standing in line at the movies.

Jake stands nose to nose with Nate, "What The Fuck Are You Doing?" Each word is its own sentence. "Get Her The Fuck Out Of Here Now."

The girl looks like she is going to burst into tears as Nate takes her hand and leads her away.

Jake watches them go, his arms stiff at this side. When he is sure she is gone, he spins around and points at me. "What the hell is he doing? What is he thinking? That's it. That's it. He's gone."

"Jake," I take a breath, smelling the expensive perfume that encompasses the clothes in the suitcase. "He's just not himself lately."

"Well, then, who the fuck is he?"

"Listen, I can't tell you what's going on, but trust me, he's going through a bad time right now."

"Because he lost his gun? Because he did something idiotic? Because he got his hands slapped by his father and uncle? That excuses his behavior?"

I cross the room and grab Jake's shoulders and hold him still until he is forced to look in my eyes.

"Remember what you said to me? We all have things we kept hidden? Nate is dealing with something right now, something from his past. You know I like Nate, but you also know that I'd never try to justify his carelessness unless I thought there was a good reason. I'm telling you, there is a good reason. Trust me on this."

His eyes narrow, his nostrils flare. I feel like I'm in a cartoon movie and Jake is going to morph into a lead ball and bounce off the walls.

"Jake. Please. I'm asking you, trust me. I don't ever ask that of you."

I feel his shoulders relax.

"Well then, you better talk to your boy and get him straightened out."

Luke appears in the doorway. "Everything okay?"

I let go of Jake and look up at Luke, "It is now."

This is what I do…at one in the morning, as a golden moon swoons in the night sky, I make bread.

It was one thing that my mom insisted on teaching Grace and I. How to make holiday bread; a recipe that has been handed down for generations. Because of the work it takes to make and its unusual sweetness, it's bread that, growing up, we only had on the eve of Christmas and Easter morning. But I find I make it whenever I need comfort.

"Where ever you go in life, what ever you do, you will always have this to tie us together. When you're feeling like you need the biggest hug you've ever needed and I can't be there physically, I will be there when you bake Holiday bread."

And so I mix the ingredients; the sugar, the flour, the oil, the yeast. Moon glow illuminates the white tiles in the kitchen and the glass bowl my hands are entrenched in.

I can smell it already. The yeasty sweet scent clings to the air and tries to shove away the horror that is pushing me into darkness.

I try to keep the images away…the woman with the soft face and terror filled eyes. The way she fell to the floor…skin so creamy white…like a snowflake falling from an overburdened cloud.

The bad thing about making bread is that you have to give it time to rise. I put it on the counter. A yellow towel covers the bowl. I slide open the screen door and sit myself down on the back deck.

From somewhere in the distance, laughter. Drunk laughter. There is a bar not too far from my home. During the summer it is not unusual to hear sounds other than the wind tugging at the trees, an owl in search of company. As the night gets later, the morning gets early, and 'last call' arrives, shouting, sometimes angry, sometimes joyous, sometimes incomprehensible, slips in through the window screens and tugs me out of a sound sleep.

"I love Andrew!" A girl's voice trills through the muggy air.

I wonder. Will the girl who loves Andrew be climbing in her car, Jack Daniels the only companion to help guide her home?

Perhaps she is sliding into a passenger seat, Andrew at the helm. Maybe Andrew will be sober. Probably not.

So if Andrew has half a load on when he climbs behind the wheel, and if the girl knows this, even in her drunken state, she knows she risks the worst outcome. He could crash and send her head first through the windshield. She knew when she started drinking that if she didn't stay rational, she could end up regretting this night and her actions for the rest of her life.

I check my watch. It's time to punch down the dough that has risen to the top of the bowl. Cover it and let it rise for another thirty minutes.

As my fist collides with the elastic bubble, I envision my mother leaning against the counter, her tan arms crossed against her chest. She would be studying me closely with round aqua eyes that can read words that are thought but not spoken. She would never point out my mistakes; she would never lay down guilt, hoping to trip me. All she would say is "I love you. No matter where you go in life, no matter who welcomes you with open arms and who turns against you, I will always think you are one of the most special people on this earth."

But I don't think she ever, in her wildest dreams, imagined that I would kill any-one in cold blood. Perhaps she'd be able to rationalize my actions in her mind. Per-haps she'd tell me, "I don't approve, but I understand."

Yes, that's what she'd tell me if she were standing here.

I place the towel over the bowl once more and retreat back to the deck.

Sirens pierce the air now. Fear seizes me, but only for a moment. I know better. If they were coming for me, there would be silence. That's the way they do those sort of things. Surround the house, guns drawn, dressed in black, barely breathing.

An ambulance wail joins the shrieking police cars. I wonder about the girl. Per-haps she's been in an accident. Her giddiness replaced by stillness. She will wake up in the hospital. Her future once filled with possibilities now bleak and heavy as this sum-mer heat. And she will blame herself. "I shouldn't have got in the car. I shouldn't have been drinking so much. I should have known better." Her family will protest, "No, no, it's not your fault. You were in the wrong place at the wrong time." But in the back of their minds they will agree with her. She knew what she was doing when she walked into that bar and didn't stop after the second drink soaked her sensibilities.

The woman in Wentworth's apartment, the woman I killed…she had to be aware of his transgressions. Which meant that she forgave his sins or refused to acknowledge them. Either way, her being there was much like the drunk girl. She knew there was danger in what she was doing. She knew darkness surrounded him. Yet she chose to be there, chose to cross that line. This knowledge gives me comfort.

What I know for sure: there are children in North Twilight who can close their eyes and sleep for the first time since coming into contact with Wentworth. There are parents who feel like someone has lifted the weight of the world off their shoulders just a bit. And there are children who don't know it, will never know it, but they have escaped the future grasp of Wentworth.

I am not happy about what I did today. I would change it if I could, but I can't. It wasn't the right thing, but it wasn't completely wrong either.

Detective Bennigan
August 10, Saturday.

I am in the shower, Luke's shower, when there is a knock on the door.

"Yes?" The water caresses my shoulders. I've only had two hours sleep, but feel as if I'm more awake than I have been for months.

"Can I come in?"

Well, why not? He's seen every inch of my body and seemed pleased by it.

"Sure." I turn off the water and climb out, wrapping a thick white towel around my body.

I had climbed into my own bed at midnight when two hours later, the phone screamed at me and I answered with dread. It had been Luke.

"Can you come over?" He had asked softly.

The blue numbers on the digital bedside clock read 2:15.

"Now?"

"Maggie, I've been lying awake, thinking you should be with me. I can't get you out of my head. Working with you and watching you and not being able to have you is driving me crazy. This case is making me nuts. I have all this energy and no where to spend it."

By 2:45, I was in his bed, our arms and legs twisted together like paper clips; thinking if this was my reward for going without all those months, it was well worth it.

Luke hands me a crystal flute glass, "Champagne." He grins lazily and kisses my damp neck.

"Wow. I'm impressed." I take a sip of the sweet bubbly.

"Steaks on the grill. Not sure how you like yours."

"I'm really impressed."

"So am I." His eyes slowly travel down my body.

He starts to pull the towel away when the phone interrupts.

"Ah...damn," he places his champagne on the sink top, "could be the station."

He picks up the extension in the bedroom. As I get dressed, I can't help but overhear his conversation (as I press an ear to the door).

"Hello?" A pause, then his voice drops a few octaves.

"This isn't a good time." Irritation. "There's nothing to talk about. It's done. It's over."

My heart sinks. Luke collects women like women collect shoes. He probably gets these kinds of calls once a week.

I'd made my share of 'can't we try this relationship ONE MORE TIME' to men who I thought I'd be better off without, and then once I was alone, missed the very things that had annoyed me so. The way they sang off key to Elvis. The way they threw wet towels on the bathroom floor. The way they scraped their plates clean of every possible morsel of food.

"How do you like your steak?" He asks after hanging up.

"Umm, well done I suppose." I look at my reflection in the mirror. Flushed cheeks, sad eyes.

"Old girlfriend. Nothing to worry about."

I put my hair in a ponytail. Easy for him to say. I can feel myself falling...and I don't want the landing to shatter my heart.

"How about after dinner, we go to a movie? Anything you want, even something with J-Lo or Sandra Bullock in it."

"I don't know, Luke." I brush by him, out of the bathroom and into the bedroom where I shove last night's clothes into my duffel bag.

"We don't have to go out. We could veg out here; drink the bottle of champagne and just stare at the stars all night."

My cell phone squawks. The ringing sounds like a bird that has just found her nest picked apart by a curious child.

"Could be the station," I smile.

It is Becky.

"I need to see you." Demanding.

"Right now?"

"Yes, is that possible? It's about the gun."

"Okay, well, how about we meet at my house?" I zip up my bag and mouth 'Sorry' to Luke. He sits on the edge of the rumpled bed looking like he just found out his favorite band was breaking up.

"I'll be there in ten minutes." Click.

"I have to go. Something's up with Becky; she needs to talk to me."

He nods, reaches for my hand. "I'll keep your steak warm?"

"Luke," I sit next to him, feeling the heat of his body against mine. "do you think this is such a good idea, really? I mean, last night was so much fun. And I'm not saying we can't have fun like that again, it's just...a movie? That's like dating."

"What's wrong with dating? We are in our thirties, I thought that's what people our age did."

I couldn't very well tell him that waking up in his arms felt so right; I could easily imagine myself waking up in his arms every morning. I couldn't very well tell him that I have a tendency to plunge into a relationship and wear my heart in plain view, giving away all my secrets and all my power. I couldn't tell him I'm impatient when it came to getting things that I want. And I was beginning to want Luke for more than just a companion in bed.

I needed to have fun, *not* get involved. I had a daughter to look out for, to protect. If we became something more than a good time...Zoey would be part of the mix. Luke didn't seem like the type of man who would stretch out on the floor with a box of crayons and a Barbie coloring book.

"Nothing is wrong with dating. But we're on this case together, right? And I don't want anything to affect our ability to do our job."

"Maggie, we've gone over this."

"No, you've told me that it wouldn't change things at work. But no one can predict the future, especially not when we don't know where our feelings will take us."

I pick up my bag and start for the door.

"I'm going to stay here and wait for you. All night if I have to. This isn't wrong Maggie." He gently tugs on my shoulder just as I'm about to step out into the unforgiving light of the afternoon. "I don't beg Maggie. But I want you to know, I feel a connection to you that I've never felt with anyone else. The timing has never been right for us, but it is now. It's right in front of us."

Oh God. This guy is good. No wonder he's a lady killer. Don't fall for it Maggie. Don't do it. You're strong. Whatever you do, don't look in his eyes. Don't look at his broad chest. Don't fall for it. Don't fall for him.

"Okay, I'll be back after I talk to Becky." Wimp! I make a mental note to check for scrapped elbows and bleeding knees after the tumble I just took.

He gives me a kiss that is a promise of things to come.

*   *   *   *

Becky is in my back yard. She is sitting on one of the swings, throwing a ball to Badge who ignores me as he runs the plastic red globe back to her.

"So, what's up?" I sit on the other swing. I fold my feet on the ground, the dry grass nipping into my skin.

"Peter Wiley brought the gun over for Marty to look at. Marty was thinking of buying it. Without telling me." She throws the ball fast and hard. It thuds against the side of the wooden fence and bounces off, flying through the air at razor speed. Badge practically bends his body in half as he quickly changes direction and hunts it down.

"He ended up not buying it. Chickened out, he said. Didn't want to piss me off."

I'm relieved.

"That's good."

"Is it?" Her eyes swing and lock on mine. "Marty and I had a huge row. He left the house last night and spent the night at his mothers. I couldn't believe that he would do something like that, and he can't understand my hatred for the fucking things."

"I'm sorry." I rest my hand on her bony knee.

"And to top it all off, my best friend thought I could be a murderer."

I suppress a giggle; it does sound funny now. Outlandish. Petite Becky (who calls me in the middle of the night because there may be a ghost in her closet) on the prowl for pedophiles. Ridiculous. "You're right. I know you could never do something like that."

"I'm glad those guys are dead, but I could never bring myself to do it. I'd have so much to lose. I love my family above all else."

"I know, Becky. I'm really, really sorry."

She stands up and shakes car keys from the pocket of her shorts. "I honestly don't know which was worse. Finding out my husband was lying to me, or finding out that my best friend didn't trust me; didn't know me well enough to ask me about it right there and then. Did you tell Jake about the gun?"

"Oh, God," I stand up and grab her wrist. "No...no Beck. I didn't say anything to Jake. And I should have said something to you right then...but...I don't know...hangover, lack of sleep. And in my line of work, well, I just have a front seat to a show where husbands and wives, mothers and fathers, best friends, think they know each other so well and it turns out…they didn't know anything about each other after all."

She shrugs away from me. Her green eyes flash with anger. "That's them Maggie. That's not us. That's not me and you." She unlatches the gate.

"Wait," I grab the wooden door, feel a sharp sting as a splinter bites into the flesh of my palm.

"The sad thing is, you thought you didn't know me, and it turns out, I was the one who didn't know you." She disappears, leaving me with a dog drooling at my feet, a sliver of wood trapped under my skin, and a weeping heart.

Whether or not you have children yourself, you are a parent to the next generation. If we can only stop thinking of children as individual property and think of them as the next generation, then we can realize we all have a role to play.

—Charlotte Davis Kasl

Sunday morning. The paper is thick with colorful ads for Target, Wal-Mart, and the grocery stores. After I read that the police have no clues but are working diligently to solve the murder of Charles Wentworth, and his sister, Veronica Brooding(who had been the one to post his bail), I turn to the letters to the editor. For every three letters supporting the actions of the "Pedophile Predator", there is one letter that lambastes me.

Over a cup of coffee and a stale doughnut, I sit in front of my computer and draft my own letter.

Dear Editor and Citizens of North Twilight:

I read with amusement the letters that have been flooding the paper since the murders of T-Ray Austin, Roger Buckley, and Charles Wentworth. Letters stating, "It's about time someone protected our children, someone did something to stop the victimization of our children."

I am pleased to see that this community is acknowledging the fact that our children are suffering.

Families are being torn apart at the hands of men who molest, are convicted and released after a few years, only to turn back to their ways.

But where were these letters when the news broke about these men being arrested? No one seemed to have time to pen a letter about their disgust. No one was upset enough to demand that the prison sentences be longer, that the court needed to change the way they handled the cases, making it easier on the children who must testify; lessening their fear. Making it easier for a child to come forward and tell his story.

The laws of this country still protect those who need it the least, The Predators. The victims suffer at the hands of these men, and then suffer again at the hands of the court system. Perhaps worst of all, they suffer at the hands of the public, who turn their heads in embarrassment and shame, afraid to utter the word; molestation.

I am one person. I can't change the system. I alone can't make this world a safer place. It is every man and woman, parent or not, who must take a stand and demand that these criminals, these degenerates of society, are severely punished quickly and harshly. It is up to each person to look out for the children of this world. They will look out for us someday. They will protect us someday. Each child is not his parent's legacy; each child is a legacy to you, your neighbor, the cashier at McDonald's, the saleswoman at Macy's, the Fed Ex driver…each of us shapes a child, whether we know it or not.

I am not advocating for each of you to take a gun and hunt down pedophiles; I'm asking that you refuse to let these vile men prey on our children. I'm asking that each of you take a responsibility to protect our children; to keep them safe, and to make it impossible for anyone to take innocence away from our children.

Take the energy that you had to create a letter to the editor and sing my praises, or that anger you had to rage at what I've done, and funnel it to the politicians, to the people who can make a difference. It has to start with you.

I'm truly sorry for the death of Veronica Brooding. Just as I don't wish innocent children to suffer needlessly, I never intended to harm someone that didn't justly deserve it.

I reread the last two sentences. Highlight the words, and cut them. I sit and stare at the letter until my legs fill with prickles from lack of circulation. Before I print out the letter, I paste the last two lines back in. It doesn't seem right not to mention her. I know my apology doesn't justify her murder, but it makes my soul feel somewhat lighter.

Detective Bennigan
August 10, Saturday evening.

I clean my house. I line the Clorox, Tilex, Scrubbing Bubbles, and Windex on the counter where they wait for me like soldiers ready for battle. I put some Tom Petty, Bad Company, Melissa Ethridge and Toby Keith on the stereo and blast it. I'm singing my heart out while I scrub things I haven't scrubbed in years; floor boards, the top of the refrigerator, the spot around the base of the toilet that always makes me gag. The fumes make me giddy and out of breath. I shut off the air conditioning and shove open the windows. Storm clouds have gathered together like an army, waiting for the signal to strike. After the dishes have been soaked and scoured and put away, I pour a glass of white wine, check my cell phone to make sure the station hasn't called, and hope that Becky *has* called to say; "Sorry" or "I understand" or "I love you".

The only number on caller id is Luke's. Three times. No messages. I rub the compact silver phone between my fingers, which are turning pruney from hot water and cleaning solution. I still have three loads of laundry to do, Zoey's room to tackle, and a slew of bills that need to be paid. It's not often that the mood strikes me to clean, so I turn up the music just a bit louder, pour another glass of wine, and break out a new roll of paper towels.

Rain begins to lash against the screens; a roll of thunder shakes the house. I turn the stereo off and listen to the drumming on the roof. I sit by the window and breathe in the sweet smell of rain.

I've always loved storms. Watching the way the sky cracks open for the briefest second as lighting parts the darkness. No matter how fierce the winds, how loud the thunder, I've always found storms soothing.

This moment though, is meant to be shared. Someone next to me to count off the seconds between the explosion of lightning and the roar of thunder.

I call Luke.

"How do you feel about dogs?"

"I love dogs, why?"

"Would you mind if I brought Badge with me? Or would you like to come over here?"

"Bring Badge over. I'd love to show him around."

"You don't want to come here?" I shimmy out of my clothes in my new sparkling clean bathroom.

"I rented a few DVD's, iced the champagne, kept the steaks warm, and whipped up some strawberry shortcake."

"You made strawberry shortcake?" I frown in the mirror. I like a guy who can cook, but not a guy who Emeril's me in the kitchen.

"Honestly? I ran up the street to the bakery."

"I'll be over...we'll be over in half an hour."

$$*\qquad*\qquad*\qquad*$$

Two o'clock in the morning and I'm sandwiched between Luke's bulky body and Badge, who has managed to charm Luke into allowing him to climb into bed.

I nudge Badge; he doesn't move. I shake him gently. He offers a snore in response. I climb over him and slide out of bed, tiptoe out into the hallway and into the kitchen. My head is slightly achy, my mouth dry from too much champagne. In the fridge I find a glass pitcher with pink lemonade. A quick glance around the doorway assures me Luke is still fast asleep. I drink from the side of the pitcher, the glass lip cool against my mouth. Luke keeps his house cool enough to please a polar bear. My toes are so cold they're turning blue.

The storm passed hours ago but the rain loiters. I ease out onto the enclosed porch, carefully closing the screen door. The moon is tucked behind a thick sky. The warm air hugs my chilled body. I put the pitcher of lemonade on a white whicker table and settle into a matching rocking chair. I still smell Luke, even out here. His scent lingers everywhere in the house. It is soothing yet energetic.

A familiar sound tugs at my ear and tickles my brain awake.

The noise is coming from the living room. I wind my way round the furniture, the coffee tables, the potted plants, two of which Badge overturned causing Luke to laugh and me to apologize profusely for half an hour.

It's my cell phone, alerting me that I have a voice mail. It must have fallen out of my jeans when I slipped out of my jeans and landed on the couch, naked cept for Luke's cloak of skin over mine.

As I bend over to pick it up, my foot accidentally kicks it under the couch.

Badge has revived himself and I can hear his nails tapping against the hardwood floor. I reach under the couch and the first thing I feel is a smooth thick book. The second thing I touch is my cell phone. I retrieve both items.

The book is a black photo album. I open my phone and dial my voice mail while I flip the cover of the album open, hoping to find pictures of Luke as a skinny, gangly boy with zits on his chin. Hoping *not* to find semi nude pictures of his ex-girlfriends.

"Maggie," The message is from Jake who is hollering into the phone, "I'm a dad. Sara Kate arrived at 11:32 tonight. She weighs 8 pounds on the nose and is gorgeous. Lucy is doing well. She pushed five times, didn't yell at me once, and said she's ready to think about having another one."

I smile into the phone; Jake hasn't been this happy since…damn, since he found out Lucy was pregnant.

"I'll be at the hospital if anything comes up with our case." Jake adds.

The man never gives it a rest.

There is a newspaper article on the first page of the album. It's about the murder of T-Ray Austin. As I flip through the rest of the pages, I find they all have to do with our Pedophile Predator.

I scan the articles quickly, most of them I've read. Why would Luke have this hidden under the couch?

"Maggie?" Luke's voice jolts my arms away from the album. The shock of his voice throws my balance off and I fall back on the floor, grabbing the space over my heart to make sure it doesn't leap out of my chest.

"Jesus, Luke, you surprised me."

"Sorry," he laughs. "I woke up to find not only had you left me, but apparently I wasn't good enough for Badge either."

At the sound of his name, Badge thumps his tail on the floor and shoves his wet nose into Luke's palm.

Luke settles himself beside me.

"My cell phone was beeping and I accidentally knocked it under the couch. I found this underneath, thought it was a photo album."

Badge has folded himself next to Luke, pressing his back into Luke's side. He is giving me a look that says "Don't scare this guy off, I need a male figure in my life, and I like this one just fine."

Luke runs his fingers along the sharp edges of the page. "I collect all the information I can about the cases I work on. Sometimes, a reporter might write something that has a clue tucked into the article. Something we missed, or something we knew about, but seeing it in writing, it jumps out at me, calls attention to what I've seen but never really considered."

I nod. "Makes sense. Have any of the articles given you a new insight?"

Luke absentmindedly rubs Badge's ears. "You know, it's as if there's something there…but I can't quite figure out what it is. I'll leave it alone for a few days and then come back and reread it, and maybe I'll figure it out then."

He pushes the album toward me. "Do you want to try it?"

"Sure, but not right now." I slide it back under the couch. "I'd rather go back to bed."

"Tired?" He pulls me up.

"Sleeping isn't what I had in mind." I grab his hand and tug him gently in the direction of the bedroom.

Progress always involves risks. You can't steal second base and keep your foot on first.

—Frederick B. Wilcox

I love summer. The long days. The energy that the sun infuses. Unlike winter when the sky turns dark at 5pm and people tuck themselves inside with artificial light and comfort foods; chili, beef stew, bread slathered with butter, pot roast. During the winter, I'm in bed by 10 and every morning I have to give myself a pep talk just to push the warm comforter away from my body.

Summer, to me, has always been about possibilities; parties, pick up games of baseball, football, basketball, local fairs and carnivals, people out and out about in the neighborhood, ready with a smile and a weather report.

The park I've chosen is just outside of town. During the day, it's filled with people barbecuing, or running along the 3 mile trail that winds around the man made lake, or feeding the ducks, or playing in the wooden castle that offers many secluded spots, perfect for a game of hide and seek.

I've told Rocker78 to meet me here, inside the castle. He thinks I'm a 13-year-old girl that lives in a farmhouse not far from the park. He's from New Jersey, 30 years old, a photographer. He told me he'd give me one hundred dollars if I would meet him and lift my shirt and play with myself.

You see, I thought I might stop, give up this life. But I'm drawn to the excitement, the sheer terror at the thought of what I'm doing, the sheer terror when I'm actually pulling the trigger and then the satisfaction that overwhelms me after. I carry this satisfaction with me like a rabbit foot on a keychain.

Some of us leave small marks on this world: The cashier at the grocery store who remembers that you like plastic bags versus paper bags. The waitress that brings a glass of Diet Coke to your table as soon as you sit down. The mailman who knocks on your door and waits till you answer when he has a package for you.

Then there are the large marks people leave on the world: Singers with their sultry voices that relax or inspire. Doctors that heal. Cops that protect. Teachers that not only teach, but listen. We all have our place in this world; we all leave a mark whether or not we are aware of it.

When I pass a child on the street, I feel a kinship. As if I know them. I feel partly responsible for the innocence that sparkles in their eyes. I'm making sure I keep that glow alive. This world will knock a kid on his ass many times, the last thing a kid needs is an adult stripping away his dignity, his dreams, his belief that the world, though not always soft and cuddly, at least has the decency to keep sexuality intact until he's reached an age to make decisions without an adult promising, cajoling, bribing, or threatening.

Headlights cut through the darkness. From where I'm perched, I can see the man climb out of his car. The moon is half of himself in a cloudless sky, and the reflection on the lake creates a candle glow effect in the darkness. I can see the excitement in the man's face. The hope. He is medium everything. Height, weight, looks. A man that could easily get lost in a crowd. A man who would hold you hostage for fifteen minutes at a party, blathering about his summer vacation. The next day, you would not be able to describe any of his features or his clothes.

He climbs the six steps that lead to the oval opening in the castle. I'm pressed in a small square room immediately to the right of the entrance. I can see him clearly. I've instructed him to meet me at the very top of the castle. "Winding stairs to your left when you enter. I'll be at the top of the steps, in a tiny room that looks like a jail."

He has passed me now, taking his first step on the wooden stair. He smells like french fries and shaving cream. His hair is greasy, gleaming in the moon glow.

I raise my right arm, my left hand supports my elbow as I steady the gun.

My gun and I are friends now. I almost think of him as pet. Steadfast and true. Me and him against the world, protecting each other. At times, I feel he has a mind of his own. I can sense his excitement as I aim at Rocker 78. I can feel his distaste for this man who thinks he is going to be looking at, and hoping to touch, the breasts of a girl so young she probably still sleeps with stuffed animals, watches cartoons on Saturday morning, and still occasionally pulls out old Barbie dolls, though she'd never admit it.

The familiar boom, the tremble of my hand, the pop of skin and bone being burned and drilled.

He falls back, reaching for a rail that does not exist. In rapid motion, his legs, his back, his head, crash against the floor. I bend over him, cock my head to the side. His eye's latch onto mine, a question, unasked. My gun ready with the answer.

A final shot to the head. We are relieved, my gun and I, as we slip out into the night. I slide the gun into my waistband, pull the leash out of my pocket and start my jog up the street.

A light beam slices through the back of my legs, illuminating the freshly mown grass. The light is weak, coming from quite a distance. It takes all my determination not to turn around to see where it is coming from.

My feet pick up speed, my lungs expand, ready for the flight about to take place. I snap the leash up to my hand and wrap my fingers around it. The flashlight beam has disappeared. I hear a scream. A line of trees separate this part of the park from the parking lot where my car is waiting. I push against brittle branches, hoping my sweat pants will stay intact, hoping they will shield my skin from potential DNA traces.

It is only thirty seconds or so before I reach the safety of my car. I drive away slowly at first so as not to leave any tire tracks on the blacktop.

It's going to be okay. It's going to be okay. It has to. Justice has to be on the side of goodness. Doesn't it?

Detective Bennigan
August 13, Tuesday. Night

The only thing I love about where I live is that the deck faces a small forest; a thicket of trees maybe a mile deep, if that. Just enough to make me feel removed from the world or suburbia. The house (that I fought so hard to keep in the divorce) is too big.

The neighbors who once invited Ben and I to every barbecue, picnic, Eagle's football party, Flyer's party, don't even acknowledge me now. If I'm out watering the lawn or getting my mail at the corner mailbox, they turn their heads, as if suddenly fascinated by the dead bugs embedded in the blacktop on the road. They are all married. I'm divorced. I'm the enemy.

The night sky glitters around a half moon. Zoey has finally fallen asleep and I'm sitting on my lounge chair with a glass of wine in one hand and the portable phone in my other.

I want to call Luke. I don't want to call Luke. These past few days of working on the case, being around him, trying to stay within the bounds of co-workers when we are wearing our badges, have been torture. When our arms accidentally bump, when I look up and find his eyes steady on mine, when he smiles at me the way he smiles at no one else, it's like my skin is on fire and I need to scrub it off.

I know the drill of love. At first, it's all heady. Like the first class of champagne. You want more, more, and then after awhile, when the bubbly wears off, you wonder why you didn't stop when you started feeling a bit woozy.

Jake came back to work for a few hours Monday and today he put in almost a full day. Though the tiredness in his bones was evident by his many trips to the coffee machine, he seemed more relaxed. The Jake of last week would have been pounding his fist against the wall in frustration because we have no clues, no evidence, not one single fiber of hair or clothes. It bothered him that someone else was winning a game that he, by life's design, was supposed to be winning.

I wasn't sure if it was the lack of sleep that was tearing down his armor or if it was the fact he was now a father and something more important than the shield gleaned in his eye. The one thing that did not change, however, was Jake's lack of enthusiasm for Luke. When Jake caught the glances that Luke and I exchanged, he would clear his throat, or slam a file drawer, or slap a pen against the metal desktop.

I take a sip of wine. An owl hoots. It's comforting. I am missing comfort. I am missing Becky. The way her house always smells like cinnamon rolls are baking in the oven. The way she always has fresh sun tea in the fridge. If she were here right now, she'd fold herself in the chair next to mine, hugging her knees. She'd stare at the stars while giving me advice.

"Just enjoy it for what it is. Of course there will be things about him you won't like that you'll find out about later. Maybe he puts leftovers in the fridge without wrapping them up. Maybe he'll only wash the bed sheets once every six months."

"Maybe he'll cheat on me." I'd tell her.

"Can't you think positively, for once? Here's what you should be thinking," she'd look at me and her eyes would be ignited but her voice would be soft, "you should be thinking that no matter what happens, if Luke is mostly all good, then you will push those bad things away, or work through them. You need to let go of that perfection ideal that you cling to."

Becky has told me this often. Like a child telling his parent to quit smoking. Like a wife asking her husband to cut back on the sweets. Like a coach telling his star player to stay away from the parties the night before the game.

I know my way of thinking is sabotaging me. I know it's a problem, and yet, I can't change it. Becky says I 'won't' change it. I have tried (I really have). But it seems the more I think positive, the more bad things seem to happen. So I figure, if I expect the worst and it doesn't happen, it's a bonus.

I decide to call Luke. It's what Becky would tell me to do.

I am pushing the numbers on the portable phone when I hear the unmistakable sound of twigs breaking and the rustling of feet outside the tall fence. I hold my breath, and clear the numbers I just dialed. My finger hovers just above the 9. I ease out of my chair and place the wine quietly on the deck. My gun is on top of the china cabinet in the dining room. Unloaded.

My heart seizes when I think of Zoey curled under the Barbie sheet in her bed.

This is when being single really sucks. When there are noises that go bump in the night and I have to do the investigating, the defending, and therefore, I'm not afforded the luxury of panicking.

As I stand and back towards the screen door I see the top of a dark head that has almost reached the gate.

"Maggie?" The gate rattles.

It is Jake. I'm relieved but angry, the adrenaline that is whipping through my veins has no where to go and the sudden wall it hits makes me want to throw the phone right at the top of his head.

"What are you doing here?" I bark as I stomp down the steps and let him in.

"I wanted to talk to you." He notices the look on my face. "Jesus, I didn't mean to scare you. Did I scare you?"

"Why didn't you call?" I ignore his question.

Badge has heard our voices and his nose is pressed against the screen. He is whining in protest…wanting to join the party.

"I was just driving around. Thinking about the case. I ended up here."

"What about Lucy and the baby?" Badge escapes when I open the door, running circles around his pal, Jake, who he has not seen for some time.

"My mother in law is in town. Lucy and the baby are sleeping. My mother in law has spent the last hour trying to convince me that the baby should go to Catholic school. I had to get out of there."

"So, what's up?" My shoulder muscles deflate and I sit back down, stretch out my legs.

"How serious is this thing between you and Luke?" He asks.

I pick up my wine glass and swish the liquid back and forth. I'm not sure how to answer.

Jake walks to the edge of the deck and rests his elbows on the ledge. He gazes straight ahead at the trees that stand at attention. "I can feel the…chemistry you two got going on. Standing between the two of you is like standing in the middle of a magnetic force field. I see the way he looks at you." He makes a face as if he's just swallowed a peppermint and it's lodged in his throat. "The other day, he asked me if I thought he was good enough for you."

I squeeze the stem of the glass tightly. "He asked you that?"

"Yeah, he asked me that."

"What did you say?"

"I said if he hurt you, I'd kill him."

I smile in the darkness. It's good to have someone looking out for me. An overprotective big brother kind of deal.

"You came here to tell me that?" I ask.

He straightens his arms and grasps the railing as if bracing himself for a gust of wind.

"Luke and I actually got along really well when we worked that drug case in Jersey. He was a pretty cool guy, a lot of fun to be around. The case didn't feel so much like a case. It felt like a vacation. Two guys living in an apartment, drinking in bars all day, going to parties at night, all part of the job. Lucy and I had been married a year. Life was a little dull at home, you know? In Pennsylvania I was a married guy, going to family functions, fixing gutters and broken lawn mowers, painting. When I got assigned the job with the task force it was like I was given a free pass to be single. That was my cover; a single guy, into drugs and drinking and only looking for a good time and good money."

Badge has curled himself next to my chair, his tongue is hanging out of his mouth and his brown eyes are watching Jake.

"There were two other undercovers who had been working the case six months before we came into the picture. Max and Nicole. Nicole was posing as a bartender in one of the clubs. Max was a bouncer. Nicole was a looker; long blonde hair, legs that came up to her armpits. She was DEA. Luke was madly in lust with her. Every guy was."

The bitterness of jealousy swells in my mouth and I swallow it down. This was many years ago. Luke's past. It shouldn't matter.

So why was Jake telling me this?

"Every Wednesday night, we met Max and Nicole at a pancake house outside of town. Luke would always hit on her. She played along, but it didn't seem like she was too interested. It just made Luke pursue her more."

"Look," the hair on the back of my neck is standing at attention, "I don't really think I want to know about this. It's none of my business. If you're trying to make me not like him…"

"Let me finish." Jake raised his hand like a stop sign. "Towards the end of our tour, the guys we were investigating threw a huge party. It started on a Thursday and ended on Sunday. The bash was at a mansion that had an indoor and outdoor pool, a movie theater, and a recording studio. There was an endless supply of drugs, food, and booze. Nicole and Max were there."

Jake was getting ready to lay something on me, something I wasn't going to like. I thought about stopping him, stopping him because what he was going to say was going to change something in my life. I didn't want any more changes.

"Nicole cornered me in one of the upstairs bedrooms the first night. We'd been drinking, not too much; we had to stay somewhat sober. She said Luke had

come on to her a little too strongly. She said she didn't mix business with pleasure. I told her I understood, and I'd talk to Luke for her. I'd tell him to back off.
And then...she kissed me."

The vision of Jake being pawed by some hot looking blonde fills half the
screen in my mind. A picture of Lucy sitting at home, waiting and worrying
about Jake fills the other screen. I envision Jake pushing the demanding woman
away, blushing all the way down to his toes and apologizing, "I'm flattered
Nicole, but I am married."

"So that's why you and Luke don't get along? Because Nicole liked you and
not him?" It didn't make much sense.

"No, it didn't bother Luke at all."

"I don't understand."

Jake shakes his head as if there is a bug buzzing dangerously close to his ear.

"Because he knows. Every time I see Luke it's like a slap in the face. I try to
forget about it, put it behind me, and then I see his face. Just like when he walked
in that bedroom."

"What do you mean? Luke saw Nicole try to kiss you?"

Jake's shoulders roll forward, his voice is caught between a choke and a sob.

"Maggie...Luke walked in on us when we were in bed...having sex."

"What?"

The pedestal under Jake crumbles before my eyes. "You...you cheated on
Lucy?"

Perfect Jake. Perfect Jake and Lucy. Him calling her twice a day, cooing over
the phone like a damn pigeon. Jake who doesn't notice girls with tits the size of
melons. Jake who picks up flowers for his wife twice a month for no reason other
than to "keep the romance alive". I have hoped and prayed that there is a duplicate of this man standing before me. Maybe not quite as anal, but a man who
loved completely and honestly and had eyes for no one but the one he had
pledged his life to. Becky had promised me there were more men like Jake in the
world. Good looking, honest. Honest above all else. Ethical and True.

I walk over to him; anger is spilling out of my pores and burning my vision.

"You're a fucking mirage Jake. A fucking phony." I jab him in the chest. "You
act like you're so damn holy. Jake Buchanan does no wrong. Jake Buchanan plays
by the rules."

"I do play by the rules Maggie, you know that. I screwed up. Once. And I
learned my lesson." A line of sweat glistens across his forehead. "I can tell you, it
changed me. I honor my vows every day. I think how lucky I am even when Lucy

bounces a check, or stains the couch with fingernail polish, or throws out half a carton of milk because it's within two days of expiring."

"Why? Why are you telling me this now?"

An animal screeches in the forest. Badge scrambles to his feet, his body frozen, ears back.

I search Jake's face for the answer and then realization squeezes my stomach, forcing air out of my lungs.

"You were afraid that Luke would tell me about your affair."

"It wasn't an affair. It was a fifteen minute mistake."

"Jesus, I don't need details." I cover my ears. "It's like imagining my father having sex with my mother. Gross."

"You're right. I never would have told you, told anyone, if I thought my mistake was still in the past. I just...I didn't want you to find out from Luke."

"You underestimate Luke. I don't think he'd ever tell me. For as much as he seems to be a player, he also seems very honorable."

My cell phone rings. The screeching animal has quieted. Badge lies back down. Jake picks up my wine and drinks it. I sigh when I recognize the number.

*   *   *   *

Half an hour later, Ben is watching Zoey, and I'm standing toe to toe with Todd Browning at the Castle Park.

"This must look really bad." Todd whimpers.

"It just depends on your story Todd." Normally, I might have had a sense of humor; normally I might have tried to make Todd feel comfortable, but I'm still reeling from the secret that Jake has pummeled me with.

"I was over there," Todd points through the trees. I can't see the parking lot but I'm familiar with the place, having made out with my share of boyfriends when I was in high school. "The guy I'm seeing...Harry," Todd leans down and whispers in my ear, "he's married, don't tell anyone, please". He straightens up again. "Harry and I were having a fight and I grabbed the flashlight and told him I was going for a walk. I'm almost through the trees when I hear a 'pop'. I see the dead guy right away, then see a guy running. I shine my flashlight on him. And then I run back through the trees and tell Harry what happened. He calls 911, but says he has to leave because his wife will cut off his nuts if she finds out he's gay."

"And he leaves you here?" I don't doubt his story. But I'm finding some of the details hard to swallow. No pun intended.

"My car was parked next to his. I left when he did, waited at the entrance to the park and after the first cop drove in, I followed."

"You're *sure* it was a guy?" I ask.

Todd frowns and leans to the left of me, squinting in the direction of the crime scene. "I think some of your cop buddies are fighting."

"What?" I spin around just as the sound of arguing voices reach me.

Nate and Jake are exchanging words. Again.

Jake reminds me of one of those toy figurines with the plastic suction cup on the bottom of a spring. You push it down and after a second or two it pops straight up in the air. Jake is actually hopping mad.

Nate is standing with his arms at his sides. Barely blinking. Three guys in uniforms swarm around them.

"I'll be right back. Don't go anywhere."

During the short walk down the small, sloping, hill, Jake quiets down and returns to the castle. Nate stares at the ground as he heads my way.

"What happened?" I step in front of Nate.

"I accidentally moved the body. I was dusting for prints and moved the guys arm cause I thought I saw something...an oily fingerprint. Then I forgot the position the arm was in."

I shrug. "Lee should have it on film, right?"

"Wrong. Lee was in his car getting the film. He hadn't taken any shots yet."

"Oh."

"Yeah. Jake told me to leave. He said he was calling in Brad Savage to do the print job. Said he's going to request a meeting with me and the Lieutenant."

"I don't know what to say, Nate."

"Hey, I'm just a fuck up, you know? I haven't been sleeping well lately. Fucking up left and right. I can't even blame him."

"Maybe this is for the best, then. Get some sleep. Take some vacation time."

"I won't have to. I'm sure I'll be suspended again."

"I'll talk to him, okay?"

"Whatever." Nate slides past me and heads to his car.

The night feels as if it is stretching itself longer and wider and from where I'm standing now, it's going to be a long road until the light of day sets things right.

There is always one moment in childhood when the door opens and lets the future in.

—Graham Greene

I find sleep elusive these days. The only things my mind can concentrate on are those damn infomercials. I could be the encyclopedia of Infomercials. Ask me anything about Nads, the George Foreman Grill, the Perfect Pancake Pan.

Tonight, though, I have a magical pill. Ambien. I finally broke down and went to the doctor I've been seeing since I was sixteen. He assured me Ambien would have me sleeping like a baby with no groggy morning side effects.

At ten thirty, I pop the small white pill. Wash it down with a glass of water. I settle myself on the couch with a thin blanket and a pillow. For some reason, I haven't been able to feel comfortable in bed. For some reason? Actually, I know the reason. I want to be positioned in the front of the house. A few feet away from the door. Where I can hear the muffle of a car engine as it stops at the curb. The approach of footsteps. The cocking of a gun.

This last time out…the paper, the news station had reported an eyewitness to the murder. That's all the information that was forthcoming. I had screwed up. Again.

I've never been a huge believer in signs, or fate. Until now.

And I've never been wishy washy. Usually, if I make up my mind about something, I stick with it. I need to lose a few pounds? I step up my workout, curtail the junk food. I don't think twice when I walk past Durgan's Bakery and the smell of french crullers dances through the air. If I decide to take a vacation, I do a little research, quickly picking an ideal spot and even if it rains the whole time, and people are rude, and luggage gets lost I never wonder if Florida would have been better than California.

But now…I seem to waffle. It's like a dizzying ball game of pickle…with the ball being tossed back and forth as I struggle to land on base. There are times I think, "This is it. It's over." I could just wake up in the morning (after my two hours of sleep) and begin my day like I used to begin my day. I could end it now and return to normalcy.

And then images flash in my mind. Statistics. There is one child molester per square mile. In his lifetime, a pedophile will have molested 380 children. In California alone, there are 63,000 convicted first time offenders. The average molester only spends 2.7 years in prison.

And then there is Rachel's story. A girl I knew in college. We had gotten smashed on grain alcohol at a Halloween party at one of the Frat houses. Somehow, we ended up in the backyard, taking turns throwing up in bushes that lined the property. After what seemed like an hour of spilling our guts, literally, Rachel started sobbing.

"I know, this sucks." I had rubbed her thin back.

"It's not that," she hiccupped.

I waited.

"My Uncle Peter died in a car accident yesterday."

"Oh, God, I'm sorry."

She laughed, shook her head, her straight blonde hair twirled round. "I'm glad he's dead."

"Oh."

She dug her heels into the grass. "When I was five, we spent the summer with Uncle Peter and Aunt Clarissa. They lived right on the ocean in Cape May in an old Victorian House that creaked and moaned at night, and scared me to death. Eventually though, the lull of the waves would calm me down and I'd fall asleep."

I waited.

"One night, I thought I was dreaming that there was a mouse in my underpants. I woke up, startled, and there was Uncle Peter, his breath smelling like garlic and beer. His hand was in my underwear. I stared at him and he told me I was having a bad dream and he was making me feel better. Not to tell anyone. Then he asked me if I wanted to go to the amusement park on the boardwalk in the afternoon. He told me about all these rides, cotton candy, and funnel cake. While he was talking, his hand was still in my panties. I was so confused. Here he was being nice to me, yet, it didn't seem right, what he was doing. And his breath was making my stomach ache."

"That's horrible." I didn't know what to do. I pulled my arm away from her back. Not sure exactly how she felt about physical touch. Did I want to hear this? I barely knew this girl, and yet, I needed to hear it. She needed someone to listen.

"Oh, it gets better. I tell him, yes, I would like to go to the boardwalk and he pulls out his…you know…and tells me to pet it like it was a bunny rabbit. It was disgusting. This long, hot, pinkish thing bobbing in the air. Smelled like sweat. I wasn't sure what to do, you know? I knew privates were privates. I knew my mom and dad got mad when I didn't listen to adults, and this was my Uncle Peter. On the three hour drive to his house, my mother kept saying, "Isn't it so sweet of Peter to let us spend the summer with him? We're so lucky. He's always been my favorite brother." So I did what he wanted, and I kept gagging. A door opened somewhere in the house and he promptly put himself back in his shorts, withdrew his hand. Then he told me if I said anything to anyone, he'd have to ask us to leave."

"So, you didn't say anything." I felt like I was going to puke again.

"Oh, I did. The next morning…I didn't sleep the rest of the night. I stayed awake with the covers pulled to my chin, holding my breath, watching the door. Anyway, I snuck into my parent's room as soon as the sun rose. Told them the whole story. My dad was ready to beat the crap out of Peter, my mom said maybe I had dreamed the whole thing."

"And then…"

"There was a confrontation. Peter denied the whole thing. Said I had a vivid imagination."

I picture the scene; confused, angry adults, standing around a dining room table. Family member pitted against family member. A small girl clutching a teddy bear, eavesdropping on the hallway steps.

"We packed up, drove back home in deadening silence. I kept crying because I wasn't sure why my parents were mad at me. I thought I'd done something even more rotten than what Uncle Peter had done. That whole summer, I woke up in the middle of the night and heard my parents arguing. I knew it was about me and what had happened.

When I was sixteen, I was digging through my mom's closet for a sweater I wanted to borrow and found a stack of letters and postcards from Peter. I was so hurt. She'd been corresponding with him all those years. I felt betrayed."

My heart was breaking in a million pieces for this girl I barely knew. What to do, what to say?

"That's so fucking shitty," I tried.

*"My mom died a year later. Breast Cancer. I was happy, glad, that she was dead. Now **that's** fucking shitty."*

I never forgot Rachel's story. I carried it with me and whenever I felt like life had wronged me in some way, her story immediately surfaced and my problems were placed in the proper light. Not such a big deal after all.

The Ambien is starting to take effect. I feel relaxed, somewhat woozy. My head feels too heavy for my shoulders. I pull the blanket around me, nesting in the couch, preparing myself for the Godsend of sleep when the 11 o'clock news begins.

"This breaking story just in to Action News." The anchorwoman with eggshell white teeth announces. "A teacher at the Little Shepherd daycare center in North Twilight has been charged with molesting two children in his care. Hayden Eighenberg has been charged with the alleged crime. He was taken into custody at 7pm this evening, arraigned in front of Judge Clemmer. Eighenberg posted bail which was set at 10,000 dollars."

Disbelief and anger pound the fog that is shrouding my brain. I struggle to sit up and listen to the rest of the news story but the Ambien is too strong. As I close my eyes and give into the darkness that is beckoning, I know one thing for sure. This is it. The last sign that I need.

Detective Bennigan
August 16th, Friday. Morning

"Look Todd, no one is saying that you are the Pedophile Predator. It just seems very coincidental that you discovered the first body and witnessed this last murder." I am hunched over my desk phone, talking quietly.

"So, do I need a lawyer or not?" Todd's voice is so high and distraught I envision phone lines sparking.

"I shouldn't even be talking to you like this, Todd. Okay? It can never hurt to have a lawyer just in case."

"You think I'm a killer. My God Woman, I once threw up because I accidentally stepped on a caterpillar and its green guts squished all over the cement. Oh, I'm feeling nauseous now just thinking about it. Hold on, I have to put my head between my legs."

I roll my eyes and throw a few Cheetos into my mouth, munching loudly.

Ever since I'd interviewed him, he called me every day, worried we thought he was the Pedophile Predator.

"Okay, I'm back. Detective, I don't even know any lawyers. Well, I know one, but he's not talking to me anymore since I told him he needed to consider waxing his back once a month."

"Look, Todd. You can't keep calling me like this."

"So, you're saying I should be worried?" His voice cracks. I can hear the tears in his eyes.

"No, Todd. I really don't think you have anything to worry about. Okay?"

"So you're saying I could leave the country?"

A pair of cowboy boots blocks the spot of floor I'm staring at. Luke. He's the only man in the state of Pennsylvania who can get away with wearing shitkickers.

"Don't leave the state without telling me, okay? And don't read into that. I have to go."

"But Detective…"

I hang up with his whiny protest ringing in my ear.

Luke hands me a white, waxy, bag and a Styrofoam cup of coffee that smells like vanilla.

"Wow, what's this for?" Inside the bag is a corn and blueberry muffin.

"I just thought, you know, you were so upset last night when the story broke about the day care center…maybe you could use a little pick me up."

I lean back in the chair, my appetite crushed as I remember that not so many hours ago I had called Luke in a fit of angry tears when I found out about the molestation allegations hurled at the daycare worker. "We almost sent Zoey to the Little Shepherd, but they had a waiting list," I'd told him.

Luke had sympathized. He had listened. He had offered advice. But as helpful as he was trying to be, it didn't feel right confiding in him. Luke didn't have kids. I knew I should be talking to Becky, but I was afraid to call her. If she gave me the cold shoulder, it would have crushed me. I tried calling Ben at work, but he was out on a house fire.

"That was an interesting phone conversation you were having." Luke sits on the edge of my desk.

I take a sip of coffee. "Were you eavesdropping?"

"I'd never admit if I was." He breaks off part of the crispy muffin top and tosses it in his mouth.

"Don't tell Jake, cause he'll freak," I lower my voice. "It was Todd. He's spazzing out. Worried we're gonna break down his door in the middle of the night and catch him in the buff…" I stop and consider this. "Actually, he'd probably like to show off his goods to a bunch of cops."

"He thinks he's a suspect?"

"He's very worried he's a suspect. He calls me everyday and asks if he should hire a lawyer."

Luke breaks off another piece of muffin top, "Interesting."

"Hey, is that my muffin or your muffin?" I pull it toward me. "Why is that interesting?" I ask, a protective hand over my breakfast.

"Well, I pretty much ruled him out. He doesn't seem that bright. Background check was spotless. But it's odd that he's so worried."

I shake my head. "Nah, he's just a guilt ridden person. I know what it's like. Once I was working the snack stand for a church carnival. There were three other people working it with me. People came and went the four hours I was there. At the end of the night, they discovered someone had stolen the money they'd put aside when the register got full. I spent a week worrying everyone thought is was me. I was so relieved when they finally caught the person who did it."

"Cute story. But I think maybe we should look into this Todd guy a little more."

"Great, you sound like Jake now." I push the muffin back.

"That's not such a bad thing."

I bit my bottom lip. I was still shell shocked over Jake's confession of infidelity.

"Zoey spending the night at her dad's house tonight?" Luke asked as he slid off the desk.

"Yeah."

"Would you care to sleep over my house then?" He asks quietly.

"Oh, I suppose." I shuffle papers on my desk, trying to suppress the huge grin tugging at the corners of my mouth.

The intercom buzzes, "Maggie?"

"Yes, Tom?"

"You have a visitor in the lobby."

Oh God. Was it possible that Todd could make it to the station so quickly?

"Who is it?"

"Becky."

A thousand images run through my mind. Susan fell and broke her leg. Marty had a heart attack (he's been taking high blood pressure pills for two years now, his father had two heart attacks at age 35). Becky has cancer and is going to die within six months. One of Becky's parents had a stroke.

"I'll be right out." I stood up, feeling a bit disoriented, as if I'd just walked through a black cave and suddenly found myself outside, blinded by sunlight.

"This is good, isn't it?" Luke asks. I'd told him Becky and I had had a fight, though not what it was about. He never pressed for details.

"I don't know."

"Don't forget our meeting with the Chief in ten minutes."

"Okay."

I take the elevator down to the first floor. The air-conditioner is working overtime now, as if to prove its worth, and the station feels like Antarctica yet I can feel the sudden wetness of sweat rings staining the armpits on my shirt.

She was staring out the front window, her back facing me as I pushed open the door to the lobby.

"Maggie!"

Her face is a mixture of relief and angst.

"Becky. What's wrong?"

"This fight between the two of us. It's stupid. I've missed you so much."

She touches my arm as if to make sure I'm flesh and bone. "When I heard the news this morning story about the Little Shepherd daycare…I thought of how close you came to sending Zoey there. I knew you must be a mess."

I throw my arms around her. We share an airport hug. The kind of hug that says, "I'm going to miss you so much while you're away." Or, as in this case, the kind of hug that says, "I'm so glad you made it back. I never thought I'd miss you as much as I did."

Tom is watching with enthusiastic eyes.

"God, Becky, you don't even know the half of everything going on. You have no idea how much I've missed my best friend."

"I've had no one to call and give updates on the Westerfield case." Becky glances around. "What's going on with this guy from the daycare?" She asks in a hushed voice.

"My friend from the SVU said the guy has strong community ties to a church, a book group, and does volunteer work for Mania on Main Street. A lot of people are coming out of the woodwork saying this guy can't be guilty of anything. But up in the unit, they're positive he's gonna get put away for a few years. I didn't ask for details. I don't think I could handle it right now."

Becky shakes her head. "Marty is sick of me. I shift between talking non stop and not talking at all. I made him go swimsuit shopping with me and he ended up leaving after half an hour and waited in the car. He told me he'd rather his body be found melted into the car seats than listen to me bitch about my thighs and ass and how they don't make swimsuits that flatter anyone but anorexics."

"Marty's right, it is a bitch shopping with you."

"I can leave," she waves at the door and grins. "Anyway, after I watched the news report…well…it put things into perspective. What's really important."

I sigh and sink down on the bench behind us. "I've been thinking about what's really important too. I feel like shit knowing my daughter is being raised by teachers in a daycare center. I mean, I trust them, I really do, and I like them a lot. But, you just never know. I should be home with Zoey. Blowing bubbles outside and drawing rainbows on the driveway with sidewalk chalk."

Becky sits next to me and puts an arm around my shoulders. "Come on, Mags. We've had this conversation a million times. You need more action then you'll find staying at home. Sesame Street, pushing the swings at the park for hours at time, walking around the block seven million times while Zoey rides her

Barbie big wheel. You'd be miserable after two days, and Zoey would pick up on it."

"I don't know." But I did know. She was right.

"I was thinking about your whole daycare situation when I was driving over here. I loved when Susie was that age. I miss it. I'd love to watch Zoey during the day. Maybe you could enroll her in a few preschool classes and I'd take her to class twice a week."

"I can't ask you to do that." I tell her quietly.

"You didn't. I'm offering. I know how the guilt eats at you, and I know that you'd feel so much better if Zoey was with me." She puts her hand on my arm and squeezes gently. "You would feel better if Zoey stayed with me, right?"

"Oh, my God, yes. Yes." I'm overwhelmed. It was enough that she showed up to put the past behind us. And now this…"Are you sure, really sure you want to take on Zoey?"

"Maggie, Badge is more work than adorable Zoey. I would feel honored."

"Okay then," I lift my head up to smile at her, feeling the warmth of the sunlight on my face as it cascades through the window.

"Maggie?" Tom's voice comes over the intercom in the lobby.

His face is pressed against a pane of plexi glass. "The meeting with the Chief?"

"Oh Shit." I bounce off the seat. "I have to go." I throw my arms around her again and hug her tightly. "Thanks so much for everything. I feel like…I've just been given a second chance at getting things right."

"I'll call you tonight." She hugs back.

As soon as she pushes through the front door, I hightail it upstairs, my step is light and it seems nothing bad can possibly happen today.

It wasn't the reward that mattered or the recognition you might harvest. It was your depth of commitment, your quality of service, the product of your devotion—these were the things that counted in a life. When you gave purely, the honor came in the giving, and that was honor enough.

—Scott O'Grady

The supermarket is crowded. Not so crowded that I have to constantly say, "Excuse me" in order to make my way down an aisle. But enough that the lines at the checkout are starting to back up.

Fresh fruits and vegetables, an angel food cake, a loaf of bread right out of the oven, fill my basket. My mouth waters as I inch forward in line. Since I started my quest, food tastes differently. A single blueberry in my mouth is an explosion of sweetness. A forkful of salad is a savory kaleidoscope of nutty, buttery, cool, spicy sensations.

Of course, I have picked a line that only has two people in front of me...and it turns out to be the slowest; the cashier, a heavy woman with a thin moustache, is having trouble scanning the groceries on the belt. There is a constant "bleep, bleep" sound ringing in checkout aisle number 5.

I spend this idle time reading the headlines on the magazines, trying to keep my mind off the food I can't wait to devour.

"Another child molester bites the dust." The woman in front of me points to the newspaper in the rack.

Goosebumps prickle my arms.

"How'd they know the guy was a molester?" She is asking no one and everyone.

"He had a few convictions under his belt. Ask me, he deserved it." The woman at the head of the line, who is trying to help the cashier locate the bar codes, answers.

"They all deserved it."

"Don't you think so?" The woman in front of me turns to me. She is chewing gum that is neon green. The gum does nothing to diminish the fragrant odor of garlic forthcoming from her mouth.

I nod. "Yeah, I guess. Though some people wouldn't agree with you."

"Ah, damn civil libbers. Maybe that's why people keep getting away with crimes…they can always find someone to listen to their sob story. Bleeding heart liberals." The woman at the head of the line helps bag her groceries. I watch the a bag of pretzels, two fried chicken Swanson frozen dinners, diet ice tea, and three red apples disappear.

"Yeah, but what about that lady who was killed…that guys sister?" She loads her items on the belt; Coco Puffs, fat free Jell-O Pudding, chocolate milk, celery, grapes, three Healthy Choice frozen meals.

"Well, that I feel bad about. You know, that's a shame and all. But, here's the thing. I actually feel SAFER knowing there is a serial killer on the loose. I feel my kids have like, a guardian angel looking out for them." Money is exchanged as the lady at the head of the line glances back at us.

The second woman shrugs. "I guess you're right. It'd be great if the killer started hunting down deadbeat dads while he's at it. Maybe that would scare my ex into sending my kid some support money."

A voice, rough yet sweet, like peanut brittle, speaks up behind me, "I'd like to shake that fellow's hand is what I'd like to do."

The three of us glance over our shoulders.

The woman who spoke is as bent and frail as a dying sapling. But her watery blue eyes are sparking. "Bout time someone stepped up to the plate. I hope by the time I'm dead, this rotten world will be full of a lot less shit."

Detective Bennigan
August 16, Friday

We are lying in a hammock in his backyard. Our legs are comfortably entwined; my head rests over his heart and the rhythmic beating is comforting. The best thing about this dry summer has been the nightly show of stars against the ink black sky.

"So, you think the Chief is wrong?" Luke's voice rumbles in his chest.

"I wouldn't say wrong. I just think it's somewhat...irresponsible not to have surveillance on the daycare teacher's house." I spy the Big Dipper, the Little Dipper and a cluster of stars that resemble a VW Bug. "You agreed with him though."

"That surprised you?" He reaches down and rests his hand on the exposed part of my belly.

"I wouldn't say surprised. I just don't really agree that it would be a waste of man power."

"This guy is too smart to try anything at the house. He's thinking we'll be staking it out. Hell, he probably thinks we're gonna tail the teacher. I have a feeling he won't even bother with good ol' Hayden. Not, at least, until everyone's forgot about him."

"Maybe." I wasn't so sure. I thought putting at least one person on Hayden Eighenberg wouldn't cause any harm.

Badge sat himself by our side, poking his wet nose into my arm.

"Badge. Lay down." I pat his head. He stares at me with his Tootsie Roll eyes.

"What does he want?" Luke reaches over and rubs my sorrowful dog's neck.

"He wants to play ball. But I didn't bring any of his toys."

"I think I have some tennis balls in the shed." Luke starts to get up but I gently push him back down.

"I'll get them. You count the stars and then let me know how many there are."

The shed smells like gasoline. Though Luke's house is immaculate, his shed is quite a different story.

A little camping grill is resting on top of a rusted lawnmower. Four by fours are thrown here, there, and everywhere. Loose nails sparkle on the oil stained floor. Grimy, frayed lawn chairs are lined against the right wall. An old saw hanging on the back wall smiles at me with its dull teeth.

A red Craftsmen toolbox, the length of the back of the shed and as tall as my waist, takes up half the space.

I tip toe around, wary of spiders and insects that may or may not bite me but why take the chance? I discover greasy rags, a broken shovel, a dirt covered rake, a few bolts and a screwdriver that is bent in half. I pick this up and hold it to the gray light bulb, turning it over and over. I tuck it in my back pocket, anxious to hear the story that belongs to it.

I pick up the rusted flashlight on top of the Craftsmen toolbox, surprised to find it works, though the light flickers each time I move it. Trying to hold it steady, I shine it behind the toolbox, where there is a good three inch gap, a spot where tennis balls could easily hide.

I lean over and the light disappears. A few taps with the heel of my hand and the light shines again. Shoved behind the toolbox…a pair of tennis shoes covered with grass clippings and a dark pair of cotton sweat pants. I pull them out.

The strands of grass are brown, but not brittle. The sweat pants are black.

Huh. I try to imagine a logical reason for a pair of shoes and sweats to be crammed behind the red box. Did Luke spill gas on the pants and disrobe so as not to drag the smell into his house? I tentatively sniff the items but, because the gas smell permeates the shed, it's hard to discern where the odor is coming from.

I point the light behind the tool box again. There are two lime green tennis balls and what looks like a…snake.

I let out a blood-curdling scream and rush out of the shed, the sweats and shoes clutched to my chest.

Luke appears within seconds, Badge brings up the rear.

"What's wrong? What's wrong?" Luke grabs my shoulders, his eyes dart over my body, looking for an open wound, a jagged gash bleeding profusely.

"There's a snake behind your toolbox." I ease myself away, backing up to the patio where I'll be able to make a quick getaway inside the house if the snake decides to pursue me.

One step, slowly, second step, breath held.

Badge follows Luke into the shed of doom and starts barking.

A shiver uncurls down my spine.

Luke walks out of the shed, a black object is coiled around his hands; he is laughing.

I scream and run into the house, letting the sweats and the shoes fall from my grasp. That's it. Any adoration or lust or adorational lust I'd had stirring in my loins vanished like a witch during the Salem trials. Any man who'd chase a woman around with a snake is not boyfriend material.

I'm at the kitchen sink, splashing cold water on my face when he walks in. Badge is barking furiously. Luke's laughter bounces off the linoleum floor.

"Maggie. Maggie, look…"

I'm gripping the edge of the sink so hard, one of my nails bends back.

The coil is shiny and motionless in his hands.

It's not a snake.

Embarrassment creeps across my face. The vicious reptile is nothing more than a dog leash.

Luke grins, "It's okay."

I take a deep breath and smile. "God, I feel like such an ass."

"I wouldn't say you are an ass. But you *do* have a nice ass."

I grab it, turning it over, a smile breaks out on my red face. It is relatively new. Still somewhat stiff, the clip is shiny gold, scratch free.

"You don't have a dog." My voice is light, but underneath, I can feel the questions rise to the surface. The sweat pants, the tennis shoes with grass clippings that had been shoved behind the tool box.

"A girl I was dating used to bring her dog over. After we went our separate ways I found the leash and threw it in the shed."

"Oh."

"She was nothing like you. She was a model." He tells me in a reassuring voice.

My eyebrows high jump my bangs.

Luke slaps his forehead, "Oh, fuck. I didn't mean…You *could* be a model Maggie. You are beautiful. I meant, you don't act like a model…into clothes and shopping and designer perfumes. You're brilliant, and witty, and down to earth." He steps close to me and rubs my arms. He kisses the top of my head. "You're what every man longs for and thinks he'll never find. Strong, yet soft. Pretty but not vain. Sexy in a classy way. Smart without making everyone else feel stupid."

This feels good. Really good. His words are what every woman wants to hear, right? Yet doubt has clenched its jaw around my instincts.

"Let's go lay down. I'll give you a back rub...chase all that stress away."

He takes my hand and I follow slowly. I run my thumb over the smooth leathery leash. Todd's voice bubbles in my head. I see him standing beside me in the park, telling me what he had witnessed at the last murder scene.

"He was wearing dark pants. They were baggy, like sweats. And holding a long, thin thing in his hand, it was black or navy. It was all shiny in the moonlight. Oh, and he almost fell, like...he was running, and then slipped but caught himself just before he tumbled down."

And when we had walked the perimeter where Todd had said the perp had ran, we discovered the grass was freshly mown.

"You okay?" Luke squeezes my hand.

I place the leash on top of the night stand.

"I'm fine." I lie.

And that's the thing, isn't it. So many lies. So many secrets. People you think you know and you don't: Jake. People you doubt when you shouldn't: Becky.

My head is spinning. I stretch out on the bed. My chest feels as if there is a thick silver chain with links as big and bulky as a professional wrestlers hand wrapped around me. I could strain against it or conserve my energy and wait for the right moment to make my escape.

Injustice anywhere is a threat to justice everywhere. We are caught in an inescapable network of mutuality, tied in a single garment of destiny. Whatever affects one directly, affects all indirectly.

—Rev. Dr. Martin Luther King, Jr.

Hayden Eighenberg's house is a two story, blue clapboard, in the middle of Violet way. It is ensconced in a housing development that's probably less than a year old. The trees in front of the homes are barely more than saplings, frail and struggling in the heat. The roads are still velvety, black as coal. Driving down the street, my tires felt like they were sailing on clouds.

When I drove by Hayden's there were two news vans stationed in front of the house. The blinds were shut against the outside elements; the afternoon sun, reporters with bulky microphones and walkers with coifed ash colored hair who maintained a safe distance across the street.

Obviously today was not going to be the day. Not until a better story came along to replace the story of a daycare teacher gone bad, sending the reporters scurrying like squirrels in search of a bigger nut.

The rest of the neighborhood was busy. Middle age mothers dotted the development, pushing their kids in top of the line strollers. Young boys, wearing baggy shorts that hung so low on their hips their ass cracked a smile at anyone who was watching closely, practiced lay-up shots on the basketball court.

I'd have to try my luck when night had wrapped its cloak around the development and hustled them into bed under the guise of security while they slept.

Detective Bennigan
August 17, Saturday night.

I snuggle down next to Zoey. Her little body is stretched out on the bed, her hands curl under her chin as she blinks her sleepy eyes.

I am exhausted. I have beaten Jake, hands down, when it comes to the haggard look. Why is it that when there is something we can't have, we spend all our time thinking about it, concentrating so hard, we actually drive it away? That's what happened last night at Luke's. I wanted to fall asleep, to lose myself in dreamland. I wanted my brain to have a mini vacation from the thoughts that were over-crowding it. I had lain in bed listening to Luke's deep sleep breathing. At times I'd wanted to shake him awake envious that sleep had found him and not me. I'd close my eyes and fill my lungs with air, exhale slowly, trying to relax. Instead of falling asleep, I became so lightheaded, I thought I'd pass out. A few times I was almost there, ready to sink into never never land, but my mind would jump up and shout, "You're almost asleep!" and my eyes would fly open and chase away the very thing I longed for.

When I wasn't courting sleep, I was thinking about the items in the shed, the saved newspaper articles. Who could I tell? Not Becky. Not after the debacle with the gun. She'd think I was losing my mind. Going off the deep end. So desperate for clues, I was seeing a mirage of evidence that didn't exist.

But what if I wasn't crazy?

"I love you, my moon." Zoey smiles and squeezes my hand.

"I love you my star." I kiss her forehead; she smells of baby shampoo and vanilla spray that she'd insisted on spritzing all over her body.

She turns on her side and gazes out at the silky sky. I rest my hand on her small back, the rise and fall of each breath is reassuring, calming.

As I lay there, trying to make up for every moment I'd missed with my daughter this week, all I could think was that this was where I truly belonged. And if I screwed things up at work...

If Luke was the Pedophile Predator, I would come under suspicion for the simple fact that I was dating him. There'd be an investigation, though I'm positive I'd be found innocent. But in the meantime, while they were investigating the case I'd be suspended and so would my paycheck.

I couldn't imagine doing something different. I wasn't trained for anything other than police work. Nor could I imagine leaving it behind to work in a windowless office, the only excitement would be when the copy machine jammed or someone brought in a cake to celebrate a birthday.

In high school, I'd made spending money by waitressing at Perkins. I'd hated the way I had to flirt with the old men who's eyes and occasionally hands, groped me as I poured coffee. I was also so clumsy that the other waitress's and waiters made up the rhyme "If dishes scatter on the floor, Maggie's on the other side of the kitchen door."

The very thought that I could lose my job drives waves of panic through my body. How would I take care of Zoey? Pay the bills? Would I end up like half of my friends from college who married, had a kid or two, divorced, and then moved back home with mom and dad to save money? There was no way I could bring myself to move back in with my parents. They were awesome people, but the whole thing about being an adult is: 1) Having your own bona fide mailbox. 2) Doing the dishes when they've piled in the sink and you've run out. 3) Leaving clean clothes in the laundry basket until they become so wrinkled, you have to wash them all over again. 4) Eating cake mix from the box.

When I'm sure Zoey has safely arrived in dream land, I quietly escape.

In the kitchen, I pour myself a glass of red wine, hoping it will take the edge off the pounding energy zipping along my limbs.

I've gone over it so many times in my head. The possibility Luke could be our guy. The crimes were always committed when he and I were apart. The evidence I'd found in the garage...no matter how circumstantial. I knew if I took the shoes into the lab and had the grass clippings processed, it would tell us if it matched the grass in the park. It would be that simple. If it came back positive...then I'd have to come clean with what I knew. But the only thing that I truly knew was that Luke had tunneled his way into my heart. I didn't want to see him behind bars. Especially for doing something that I wasn't truly sure was a crime on a sort of emotional cosmic level.

My cell phone vibrates.

"Hello?"

"Maggie? It's Luke."

"Hey, I was just thinking about you." Hope he didn't ask what I was thinking about.

"Do you think I could come over for a little while? There's something I need to talk to you about."

"Umm, okay. What's wrong?"

"I'll be over in ten minutes."

I sit on the edge of the couch. In the time it takes for him to walk through the door, I drink three glasses of wine. And my nerves are so knotted and pressured, they've begun to fray.

"Hi," I stand up to greet him. His breath smells of spearmint as he bends to kiss me. Unconsciously, I turn my head, his kiss lands on my cheek.

"What's wrong?" I sink back down onto the buttery yellow sofa that I'd spent almost a thousand dollars on against Ben's advice. It was the most comfortable, pretty, piece of furniture I owned.

"That is what is wrong. Turning away from me when I try to kiss you." He paces the floor. "Ever since last night you've been distant with me. I keep going over everything, trying to figure out what I did wrong."

"You haven't done anything wrong..."

"Was it because I chased you, pretending I had a snake? I know it was a bit childish, I just thought..."

"It's not that," I could feel the heat inch around the edge of my face, spreading inward.

"What then? Because, I can tell you Maggie, I've really fallen for you, in a big way. And...it's not often...fuck, actually, I don't think I've ever felt this way, and if I screwed something up, I want to make it right." His eyes are sad; the little lines at the corners are prominent in the hazy glow of the lamp. My heart is stinging and I want to pull his face to mine and give him a reassuring kiss, put everything out of my mind. But...

"It's just lately...some things have happened, nothing to do with you..." I look him in the eye as I lie, "things that have made me question how well I really know people. And I guess that's been on weighing on my mind."

Confusion crosses his face. "Something I've done or said?"

I start to say no, then think better of it. "Is there...anything you want to tell me? Something...you're wanting to tell me but afraid of what I'll think or do?"

Okay, I'm thinking to myself. I'm an idiot. He's not going to come out and say, "Well, yes, there is this little matter of me being a serial killer. Whew, thank God that's off my chest. You won't tell anyone, will you?"

Instead, Luke drops onto the chair opposite the couch. It's a worn thing, came from Ben's parents. Something they found in the basement when trying to help us furnish our place. Faded blue, sags in the middle. Ben had no room for it in his apartment. And I couldn't bring myself to throw it out. I was waiting for a spring to bust through so I wouldn't feel so bad about kicking it to the curb.

Luke rests his elbows on his knee and hangs his head, flexing his hands every few seconds.

"I guess it's not good to start a relationship with secrets." He takes a deep breath.

The wine suddenly makes a second appearance, this time coming from my stomach to my throat. I swallow it back down and dig my fingernails into the cushion.

"Look, Luke." My thoughts are coming fast and furious, snapping like burning high tension wires. If he tells me, I'll be an accomplice. If he tells me, I'll have to turn him in, and I can't do that. Not just yet. Not now. "Sometimes, you know, we think we want to know everything. I think I want to know everything, but…the fact is, sometimes, it's better off not to know. Whatever is in front of us, well, that's what we have. Why complicate things?"

I was a fraud. Fraud! Some cop. Letting love kick my ethics right down the fucking sewer.

"No. It's only right that you know. You are one of those women who can sense when things aren't kosher. My mom is like that. She'll get a bad feeling, won't be able to shake it but can't name it, and then sure enough, something shitty will happen."

"Those sweat pants and shoes that I found in the shed…" I ask quietly. I don't want to watch his expression, but as a detective, feel compelled to observe him. Even though, I've often noticed that when people who I am close to are lying to me, it's harder to distinguish from the average Joe on the street. Because I want so bad to believe that the people I respect won't try to mislead me.

"The stuff in the shed?"

"When I found the dog leash that I thought was a snake? There was a pair of tennis shoes and black sweat pants in the shed."

He rubs his forehead. Clearly, what I have in mind, and what he has in mind, are two different things.

"Sweat pants? Shoes?" and then that AHA! moment lights his eyes. "Oh Shit, yeah, yeah. The last time I mowed the lawn, I backed into a briar bush. I went into the shed to pick the freaking needles out of my ass."

"So, you left your sweats in the shed and streaked across your yard?"

"Actually, I was commando that day. By the time I was in the shed it was night so I just sprinted into the house."

It made sense. At least, I suppose the explanation rang true for a normal person. But I was not normal. There are two sides to every story. And he could be telling me the story he thinks I want to hear. After all, he's not going to smack his forehead and say to me, "Oh, yeah. I wore those clothes when I killed that guy at the Castle Park. I shoved them in the shed and forgot about them. Thanks for reminding me."

I scoot to the edge of the couch and lace my hands together. "What is it that you want to tell me?"

His smile disappears and he leans back in the chair; his ass sinks into the hole and he's now an inch shorter. "Remember the other day…you were at my house when an old girlfriend called?"

I nod. Oh God. Please don't tell me he slept with her again. Anything. Anything but that. Please. I don't have the strength to handle it. I'll never believe in love again. Of course, if Luke let me down, if love once again waved its middle finger at me, the upside would be that I could eat all the food I craved. All the ham hoagies (extra mayo and oil) and Cheetos and Pizza Hut Pan Pizza and ice cream sandwiches, because who would care how I looked? Also, if he did sleep with her, I'd call Jake the minute he left and spill the beans about the clothes in the shed, the leash, and the newspaper articles under the couch. Any sense of protection I felt toward Luke would follow him out the door.

"Well, she called again yesterday. Said she was two months pregnant with…my…" He pulls his fingers, snapping his knuckles. Pop. Pop Pop. Pop I cringe.

Okay. I take it back. Sleeping with an ex girlfriend would have been shitty. But another woman carrying his child? Fuck. How would I ever handle that?

"It's not that bad. Well, I mean it is, but it isn't." He takes a deep breath and looks up at the cobwebs clinging to the corners of the ceiling. "She's going to have an abortion tomorrow. She called to let me know and asked how I felt and if I'd go with her."

"And how do you feel?" I was relieved and sad and a bit worried that the both of them sharing such a traumatic event might draw them back together. I'm such a selfish bitch sometimes.

"I'm…it's only been two days that I've known about it. I'm not ready to become a dad, but I'm worried I'm this horrible, rotten, person because I'm not putting up a fight, because I'm relieved she's decided to…" He rubs his forehead again.

"I'm really, really sorry." I nestle in his lap and wrap my arms around him.

We rest together for such a long time the circulation in my ass falls asleep, and I feel like there are a thousand pins prodding my butt cheeks.

"You don't hate me?" His voice vibrates through his chest.

"Of course not. I just wish there was something I could do to make you feel better."

He runs his fingers through my hair. "You've made me feel a thousand times better than I was feeling. I suppose it'll be a difficult thing tomorrow. And carrying around the knowledge that I could have been a father…"

"Time will ease the pain." I slip off his lap, kiss the top of his head. I feel a rush of sympathy for the pregnant ex-girlfriend and the sadness that will haunt her more than him.

"Do you want some wine?"

"No, I better get home. I have an early day tomorrow. I'm driving to Baltimore tomorrow. That's where she lives. I'm not sure when I'll be back, but I'll call you first thing."

"Okay, sure. Good luck." I walk him to the door. Jealousy snaps at my heels.

Outside he gives me a soft kiss on the lips, then tilts my chin up and stares into my eyes.

"Why were you curious about the stuff in the shed?"

I pull away and become interested in the buttons on my shirt. Checking each one to make sure it's in the right buttonhole. "Oh, that. You know, I guess I just pictured you having…you know, wild sex or something in the shed."

Luke smiles. "Can't say I've ever done it in the shed."

We say goodbye and I stand on the stoop, watching until his car is swallowed by darkness. It just keeps piling up, doesn't it?

Your belief determines your action and your action determines your results, but first you have to believe.

—Mark Victor Hansen

It's one in the morning. The only people out on the streets are those people coming home from the bars, or on their way to different bars, trying to squeeze the last few in before closing hour.

Of course, there are cops out, but I pass only one as I head back to Hayden's house. The cop is sitting in the parking lot of a 7-11, chatting it up with two girls, their hair so ratted and teased they look like time travelers from 1983. Or else they're from New Jersey.

As I make a right at the top of the hill that leads into the development, I notice for the first time the stone sign proclaiming "Heatherhew Village". It's nicely landscaped, with a half moon of white, pink, and purple flowers below the sign.

I drive slowly, my mouth becoming dry as I near Violet Way. My hands are slick with sweat; they almost slide off the wheel.

The six o'clock news had flashed Hayden's picture tonight. He was actually a decent looking guy. Medium build. Wearing blue jeans and a short sleeve white oxford shirt as he headed to his lawyers office. A thin face, five o'clock shadow, deep eyes, strong chin. Brown hair, kept respectively short. The kind of guy that women flash smiles at, the kind of guy that men instantly trust to back them into a parking space. And now of course, we knew, the kind of guy that kids would trust as quickly as you can say, "Want some candy little girl?"

There are street lamps on the main road in Heatherhew, but the back roads are dark with the exception of a few porch lights glowing softly.

Violet Way is lit up, however, like a circus tent. I suppose the neighbors here are suddenly afraid of things that might go bump in the night. As I let my foot off the gas and coast slowly by Hayden's house, my heart sinks.

There are two cars in the driveway, and two cars parked along the curb. Steady light burns in the downstairs windows, and behind the blinds, I can make out moving silhouettes.

I'm not sure what bothers me more. The fact that I can't pull off my plan as I intended, or the fact this pervert has friends who support him.

Detective Bennigan
August 18, Sunday.

I spent an hour at the gym. There is something about lifting weights that take the mind off places it shouldn't be. For 60 minutes, the only thing I thought about was how I was going to force my legs to press 90 pounds of steel away from my body without groaning and grunting like the steroidal hulks around me. They sounded like they were giving birth. Or having an orgasm. It grossed me out.

When I picked up Zoey from the gym daycare and saw a mother cradling a cherub faced baby, the force field that had been protecting my thoughts disintegrated into ashes. I wondered where Luke was, how his emotions were holding up. How the ex-girlfriend was doing.

I took Zoey to Barnes and Noble so she could pick out a few books and play with the Thomas the Tank train set in the kids department. As we were heading out the store, I (keeping a watchful eye on Zoey who was holding a cotton candy slushy that was piled dangerously high with whip cream and sprinkles) pushed the door open and almost crashed into a woman who was so pregnant I thought our near collision would be enough to knock the kid out of her.

That's when I decided to head to the station. Go over a few more files. Maybe there was something I'd missed.

I stationed Zoey in the dispatch office with a sheath of papers, colored pens, her new books, and told Tom (I'd bought him a cheesesteak, french fries, and the largest coke I could find) to send her back to me when he couldn't take it anymore.

"Hey, we've got food, a Bear in the Big Blue House book, and a copy machine. I'll be...I mean, Zoey will be entertained for hours. We'll be fine." Tom assured me.

I slid my ID card through the slot and was buzzed into the Detective office.

"Nate!" I was shocked to see him hunched over a computer. He'd been suspended since the Castle Park murder.

"Hey, Maggie." He looked just as surprised to see me.

"What are you doing here?" I asked as I threw my stuff on my desk.

He shrugged his tan shoulders. He was wearing a gray tank top and pair of white basketball shorts. He was so damn young and cute. "Just making sure all my reports are filed."

"Oh, well...that's good. Jake would be proud."

"Proud of what?" Jake's voice boomed behind me.

I spun around. "What's going on?" I crossed my arms across my chest. "If Lee suddenly walks out of the break room, I'm gonna be pissed that you called a meeting without me."

"Nothing of the sort. I'm just here to look over some of the pictures, go over some of Todd's statements."

"C'mon Jake. He didn't have anything to do with it." I sighed.

"I'm not saying he did, I'm just saying I'm going over his statements." He threw me the Snickers bar he was holding. "Maybe you need this more than I do. Sort of bitchy today, eh?"

Jake and Nate exchange a grin.

The intercom on Nate's desk buzzes. I hold my breath, hoping it isn't Zoey playing with the phones.

Nate slides across the floor to his workstation.

"Yeah."

"Officer Davidson is here with lunch." Tom announces, a hint of sarcasm tinges his voice.

"Okay, I'll buzz her in."

"Huh. Here to put in some extra time?" I wag my finger.

Officer Julia Davidson had just completed her rookie training. She's 5'6, lean, with shoulder length strawberry blonde hair that has a slight curl and a sweet face that had every guy rushing to be her backup on her calls. I knew the drill well. Her aura would wear off within a few months (she'd be grateful) and she'd have to call out at least twice before someone would shake off a nap in order to cover her ass.

Julia appears with a white bag from the sandwich shop across the street. When she sees Jake and I, her face turns amber.

"Maggie, your daughter is so cute." Julia stutters, making me wonder just what Nate and her had planned to do on her lunch break.

"Thanks, she takes after her dad." I pull out the Pedophile Predator files. They weren't as thick as they should be.

"Yeah, but Zoey's got her mom's trash mouth. I've never seen a three year old drop F'bombs the way this kid does." Jake grins, winking at me.

I give him the finger.

"See? It's no wonder the kid talks trash."

Nate and Julia laugh before disappearing into the breakroom.

"All right, I'm leaving." Jake sits on the edge of my desk, swinging his left leg back and forth.

"But I thought you were going to work?"

"Mags, I've been here since 8 am. Awake since 4."

"Well, you seem very chipper." I tear open the candy bar.

"And you look like shit. Too many late nights with Luke?"

"No, we rarely spend the night together. I've just had a lot on my mind."

A cloud of apprehension crosses his face.

"It has nothing to do with your...confession." I shuffle the files.

"If you need to talk or anything..."

"Thanks." I tell him with forced cheerfulness.

As he was straightening his desk, putting all his little paper clips in a plastic box and placing the pens in their rightful holders, I checked my voicemail.

"Detective Bennigan. That foxy Detective called me and I'm wondering why he's calling me when I thought I was dealing only with you. If there is something you need to tell me...I'm sleeping with all my clothes on in case you guys show up at my house and that TV show COPS is with you. Wait, on second thought, it might be more interesting if I slept in the nude. Call me."

Okay. Foxy detective. Could be Jake. Could be Luke. Could even be Nate, though he usually only handles the fingerprint end of things.

"Did you call Todd?" I ask Jake.

"Yep." He pulls his car keys out of his pocket.

"My report wasn't good enough?"

"I just wanted to hear things for myself. Your report was great Maggie. It's just...I've got this hunch."

"What is it?"

"Not sure, really. I need to work a few things out before I put a voice to what I feel. I'm not usually the one with gut instinct, that's your department. This is kind of new to me. Don't think I like it."

"No?"

"No. It's like constant heartburn, with no annoying burps."

"Let me know when you've decided if your hunch is more than just a hunch."

"You'll be the first to know. And don't be spreading it around that I got something under my hat, you know, in case it turns out I'm wrong, I don't want to look like an ass."

"Gotcha."

He grabs a notebook, says goodbye then disappears out the door.

If he suspected Luke, he certainly wouldn't tell me he had a hunch, would he? Unless he wanted to gauge my reaction…see if I knew anything.

No, Jake would never set me up.

I make my way over to the water cooler and lean down, pressing my forehead against the cool plastic while my cup fills.

Nate walks back into the office.

"That was quick," I say, keeping my head down.

"Yeah, there's a silent hold up alarm at Union National. She went as back up." He leans against my desk. "You okay?"

"Does Jake seem normal to you?"

"Like, right now, is he normal? Or was he ever normal?"

"He just seems…different."

"He's had no sleep. A new baby. A case with no clues. If you ask me, he's actually calmer than I've ever seen him."

"I know. I'm not sure if I like that." I finally raise my head and take a sip of water.

"I like this new Jake. He smiles a lot more."

"Umm. I'm not sure. The jury is still out on that one."

My intercom buzzes. "Hey Maggie, Zoey just made 100 color copies of her blankee while I was on the phone. Not that I mind, but if you could…"

"I'll be right there." I sigh. "You got any vodka hidden in your desk?" I smile wearily at Nate. This is going to be a long, long, day.

*   *   *   *

8pm. I missed a call from Luke because my cell phone was on vibrate. He left me a voice mail at 3pm. "Just wanted to let you know I'm thinking of you.

Things got a little complicated here. I'm not sure when I'll be home. It might be really late. If you don't mind me calling, leave your cell phone on. If it goes right into your voicemail, I'll know you gave up waiting. And I'll understand. I miss you. I'm so sorry." I replayed the message seven times. How was his voice? Tired? Angry? Sad? Did he really miss me? I tried to listen for sounds in the background. Music? No. Silverware clattering? No. Only silence.

For the first time in ages, Zoey has fallen asleep on the couch while watching 'The Grinch'. I carry her upstairs and tuck her in.

Downstairs, I start to pace the living room floor. Badge paces with me, thinks we are playing some sort of game. His tale wags every now and then and he looks up at me with expectant eyes. "What's next? What's next?" He seems to ask.

There is a tentative knock at the door. My heart leaps. Could it be Luke?

I throw open the door and there stands Becky.

"Hi," I'm happy to see her but I wish that Luke was behind her.

"Hey. Isn't Jake here yet?" She brushes past me, bending down to give Badge a hug.

"Jake? Why would he be here?"

"I don't know. He called me and asked if I could do him a big favor because you had to go in to work tonight. He asked if I could stay with Zoey."

As if on cue, a gray Ford Mercury slides next to the curb; Jake is behind the wheel.

"What is going on?" I stand in the doorway, watching him climb out. He waves at me.

"I don't know. I have to admit, I thought it was odd when he called." Becky stands beside me. Her hair smells freshly washed; like lilacs.

Jake starts up the walk, a relaxed smile on his face. "Hey Maggie. Get your piece, your vest and wear something comfortable. We're going on a stakeout."

"What? Where?" I knew damn well where. But I couldn't believe this was happening. "The Chief knows about this?"

"Maggie. Don't worry." He claps me on the back, "We're the lead detectives on the case. I can't go around asking everyone if I can please wipe my ass. You don't have to come with me. But as my partner, I wish you would."

I glance up at the sky. Has there been some planetary changes? Some big shifting of the solar system? Because I don't know the man standing beside me. I'd always wished Jake would be a little less cautious and now I had it. What was that old saying? Be careful what you wish for…

"Fine. I'll go change."

Upstairs, I pull on my vest and some light gym shorts and the thinnest t-shirt I can find that will fit over the vest. I stare at the phone. Call Luke? Tell him what Jake and I are up to? Warn him...just in case...

No, no, no. Phone records can be traced. A call to Luke now would make me look guilty. Before I go back downstairs, I sneak into Zoey's room and push her bangs off her forehead where I plant a soft kiss and remind myself that I can't lose this. Zoey is what is important. Being her mother. Always there for her. "You are my star." I whisper in her tiny, delicate, ear as I slip off the bed to disappear into a night that is guaranteed to be full of surprises.

Corn can't expect justice from a court composed of chickens.

—African Proverb

I drive by the house again tonight. No cars in the driveway. The downstairs is a dark as dead. Upstairs, a light glows.

It's balmy, like all the other nights have been, with one difference. An easterly breeze. People have opened their windows to welcome the change. Shutting off forced cold air in favor of something natural, if not as cooling, more comforting perhaps.

I can only hope that Hayden will follow the lead, but I know if he is smart, and that could be arguable, he will lock his windows, push furniture against the doors, knowing there's a hunt on for pedophiles and he's the new target on the range...

The windows in the front appear to be closed. But I know that the most safety conscious people are often lured by the romance of nature, the sweetness of a breeze making curtains sway. The fragrance of night sweeping through the house. Perhaps Hayden has left a window open in the back. Maybe there's one he's forgot to latch. I'll have my answer in a few short hours.

I'm feeling good. My body feels light, fueled by energy and yet...a sort of peace. As I head out of the development, a white object swoops down from the sky, almost crashing into the windshield.

I slam on the brakes, as the object, a bird, a large bird with an incredible wingspan, glares at me. Yellow angry eyes. Its beak is short and smashed against its face.

An owl. It seems suspended in front of me, staring me down. Then it lifts off and folds itself back into the darkness, making me doubt our brief encounter.

I steer the car to the side of the road in order to catch my breath. Wait for my heart to dislodge from my throat. After a few minutes, I pull back onto the road, head for home. Somewhere back in my mind, a memory. A superstition. An owl in the light of day means death is near by…but what does an owl staring you down in the dark of night mean?

Detective Bennigan
August 18, Sunday night.

Jake bought me a ham hoagie as a sort of peace offering. It would have been great except that I don't have much of an appetite and now the whole car smells like mayonnaise and onions.

We left at 8:30. It is now 10:00 and I have asked a million questions and Jake keeps repeating, "Just wait and see, I don't want to look like an ass if I'm wrong."

It feels like a game of cards. Is he testing me to see if I'm bluffing, to see if I'll fold or play my hand. The only problem is, I don't know what the cards are that I'm holding.

"What should I do about my cell phone?" I had asked when we left.

"What do you mean?"

"Luke might call me. What do I tell him?"

"Hmmm. Yeah, I could see where that wouldn't be such a good thing. But then again, you don't want to lie to him either."

He had contemplated for a few minutes, then shrugged. "Just tell him that you're with me, I'm going through something right now and you need to be there for me."

"Great."

"It's not really a lie, just a bend on the truth."

A few minutes after ten, I'm thinking the sharp pains in my gut might be quelled by eating.

"You think the hoagie is still good?" I ask.

"Yeah, it's been in the cooler." He reaches behind my seat and lifts the lid on the small blue box that we've come to refer to as the 'stakeout' fridge.

A car turns onto the street and we slouch down. As the car slowly passes us, we carefully peer through the windshield.

"It's Luke." Jake breathes. "Did you tell him we were here?"

"No, no, I haven't talked to him all day." I whisper.

"Great. Do you think Becky told him?"

"I'll call her."

After the third ring, she answers, her voice sounds like she's been snacking on gravel. "Hello?"

"Beck, it's me...did Luke call?"

"No."

I bite my lip. Luke's car has turned the corner.

"He came over though." She clears her throat.

"What did you tell him?"

"I told him you went out with Jake. I didn't say you guys were working or anything. Jake made me promise not to say a word."

"Okay. Thanks. How's Zoey?"

"Fine. Didn't get up once."

"Good. Okay. I'll see you soon, I hope."

Jake leans against the side of the door and is staring at me.

"He stopped by the house. Becky told him we went out together, she wasn't sure where."

"Ah, see, that tipped him off." He shakes his head, "You would have told Becky where you were going in case she needed to reach you and couldn't get thru to your cell phone."

"I wonder why he didn't call me?"

Jake bangs his hand on the steering wheel. "Fuck. This isn't going the way I planned it."

"Should I call him?" I ask.

"No. No. I'm sure he made us."

"I don't know, Jake. This is a brand new undercover car. And if he made us, don't you think he'd have stopped?"

"And do what? Cause a scene in front of Hayden's house? No way, Luke is much smarter than that."

"So maybe we should go?" I suggest.

He shakes his head adamantly. "No. There's a slight chance he didn't see us."

The only choice I have now is to fold my cards. "So, you think our Pedophile Predator is Luke?"

Jake frowns, cocks his head and looks at me from the corner of his eye. "Is there something you need to tell me?"

What to do. Tell him all, save my job? If I'm wrong, and point a finger in the direction of the man I've fallen in love with, it will be an ugly, ugly, scene. Tell him nothing, and if Luke is the Pedophile Predator, act stupid and hope they buy it?

I decide to ride the middle.

"Well, I found this photo album under Luke's couch. It was filled with newspaper articles and the Letters to the Editor, all dealing with the case."

"So?"

"Well, I thought it was strange. He said he likes to keep articles about cases he's working on, that way he can go back, read the stuff, and maybe find something he's missed that the paper's picked up on."

"Huh." Jake said, pushing back against the seat.

That was it? Huh?

"So, you...suspect Luke?" I ask timidly.

Jake closes his eyes. "I just had a hunch about something Maggie. I'm not saying more until I'm sure I'm right."

"I want to go home."

"Just wait."

"I feel like you're setting me up."

He twists in his seat to face me. "Why would you say something like that? Maggie, if I ever suspected you knew something, I'd come right out and ask you. I'd never set you up. You've been my partner for three years; you should know me by now."

"I thought I did, remember?" If my words were a slap, they would have left a red mark on his face.

He nods, turns back to stare out the windshield. "Fine."

"Fine."

At this moment, the only thing I know about anyone, including myself, is that I don't know a fucking damn thing I once thought I knew.

I love the man that can smile in trouble, that can gather strength from distress, and grow brave by reflection. 'Tis the business of little minds to shrink, but he whose heart is firm, and whose conscience approves his conduct, will pursue his principles unto death.

—*Thomas Paine*

Along with the breeze tonight, there are clouds in sky and they roll by the moon, dimming the shine and at times, depending on the cloud thickness, there is almost complete darkness.

The car crawls along Violet Lane. I hit the lights and park two houses away, slipping into the backyard of the house I've parked in front of. I stay low and streak across the scratchy thin grass until I've reached Hayden's yard. I've already decided, the first hint of trouble and I'm outta here. If I try the windows and they're locked, I'm outta here. There will be another time. It doesn't have to be tonight.

The windows are long, like caskets. The window on the right is closed tightly. There is a smell in the air. Like rotting apples. I press my body against the side of house, slouching along the cool siding. French sliding doors covered with thick blinds separate the windows. I turn and grasp the sleek handle and that's when I feel it; the unmistakable nudge of the barrel of a gun against my back.

My gun in tucked in the front waistband of my pants. I start to reach for it. Afraid to move too quickly, afraid to move too slowly. Afraid a bullet will be shot into my back and lodge itself in my spine.

"What the fuck are you doing?" I hear her distinctive voice. It's pissed off. It's bewildered. I give up on getting the gun, put my arms in the air. It's over. It's really over. And of all the people I never wanted to hurt, it was Maggie.

Detective Bennigan
August 18, Sunday

It's official. The circle of friends that I have, the people I thought I knew: They're all fucked up. That must mean I'm either *really* fucked up or *really* naïve. Maybe a bit of both.

I have my gun trained on Nate. I look over at Jake, wondering why he hasn't pounced on him yet. I wish I could accurately describe the look on Jake's face. It's like he's trying to decide if he should go to a frat party with the cool guys or stay and study for final exams. His hesitation has me baffled. My free hand reaches for my handcuffs when Jake finally speaks. His voice is low and rumbles like a tractor-trailer crossing a bridge.

"Run back to your car and get the fuck out of here Nate. And I mean, out of here. Out of this city, out of this state. I'm giving you the biggest fucking gift of your life, don't question it. And this better never, ever, come back to haunt me or Maggie."

Nate's arms fall to his sides. His face is void of all color and expression.

"What are you doing, Jake?" I hiss.

Jake slips his gun back in the holster under his arm. "Go, Nate. Now."

Nate hesitates.

The three of us stand frozen, less than an arms length apart.

"Put your gun away Maggie." Jake's voice sounds distant, tinny.

My arm refuses to fold...habit I suppose. It feels as if there is a brick on the barrel of the gun; my wrist trembles, struggling to keep the gun steady.

Nate takes off in a blur of motion. It's not until I see the brake lights on his car flash as he makes the turn at the end of the road that I put my gun away.

"You want to explain?" Little firecrackers are bursting in my head, sparks blur my vision. Jake has grabbed my arm and is dragging me across the yard.

"In the car." His voice is low, monotone.

I let him push my body into the car. My legs and arms have the consistency of Silly Putty. I'm sure if Jake put just the right amount of pressure on my shoulder, it would collapse into my neck.

As we pull away from the curb, I stare at the houses around us, watching for any sudden illumination of light.

"What's gonna happen if someone just saw this whole thing?" I start to hyperventilate.

"We'll just say that we were staking the place out, one of our guys was doing the same thing, making sure the house was locked up. That's it. Just tangled communication lines." Jake's voice is confident.

I tuck my head between my knees, trying to take slow steady breaths.

"What the fuck just happened, Jake? Was Nate your hunch? Or was it Luke?"

"Luke?" Jake snorts. "I never thought it was Luke."

"But Nate?" My empty Diet Coke bottle is rolling on the floor mat. I focus my eyes on it. Don't lose it now, Maggie. Don't lose it now.

"I started suspecting something was up when he showed up drunk at the second crime scene. Nate might be young Maggie, but he's not fucking stupid. Not when his dad is a councilman and his uncle is Chief of police. Then he brings his girlfriend to Wentworth's apartment?" Jake reaches over and tugs the back of my shirt, trying to lift my head out of my knees. "Just think Maggie...if we had figured out it was Nate, the case would get thrown out because he was tampering with evidence. But he also made damn sure no evidence was left behind."

The big picture is forming in front of me. Puzzle piece sliding into puzzle piece. I sit up. "Nate told me he was molested when he was a kid. That's why he was screwing up so much...because his past was...you know...haunting him."

Jake thinks about this. I notice the hairs on the back of his arms are erect, goose pimples cover his skin. "Could be...maybe it sent him off the deep end. Maybe he's extracting his own sort of revenge. Maybe not. Either way, he was trying to cover for the real reason he was fucking things up. He needed a friend in his corner, someone to buffer me. He played you, Maggie."

"I don't believe it." I lock my hands together, lace my fingers and squeeze as hard as I can, my nails biting into my flesh.

But the biggest question of all still has yet to be asked and answered.

"Why did you let him go?"

Just then, my cell phone rings.

A man's ethical behavior should be based effectually on sympathy, education, and social ties; no religious basis is necessary. Man would indeed be in a poor way if he had to be restrained by fear of punishment and hope of reward after death.

—*Albert Einstein*

I pull into a gas station that is closed for the night. I park by the payphone, and proceed to vomit what seems like every ounce of food I've ingested for the past year. Then I pick up the payphone, deposit my money, and call Maggie.

"Hello?"

"Maggie, it's me. I'm calling from a payphone. I just had to tell you I'm really, really sorry that…I didn't mean to hurt you. I…didn't mean to involve you."

"Nate." Her voice reaches through the phone like fingers, strangling my neck. "I'm having trouble believing this."

"There are times I can't believe it myself."

A black cat climbs out of a pile of tires stacked against a fence. It eyes me suspiciously as it leaps from rubber circle to rubber circle.

"Nate…remember the day you told me you were molested?"

"Yes." I press the receiver against my forehead.

"Is that what this is about? You were molested and you're seeking some sort of revenge?"

The cat is prancing toward the car. His suspicion has melted to curiosity.

It would be so easy to let Maggie believe I had been a victim. But I don't want to make things any worse for people who **have** been molested and abused. I don't want to use it as defense, an excuse, or a crutch.

"It's not revenge, Maggie. It's avenge."

Her sigh sounds like a tire that has just been stabbed by a knife. "What's the difference between revenge and avenge?"

A police car cruises by. The officer is speaking into the radio, his eyes are trained on the computer screen in the center console.

"I just got fed up. Tired of reading about the way these pedophiles defeat the system…not that there's much of a system to defeat."

"Nate." Jake's voice booms.

"Yeah?"

"Get out of town, will ya? Before I change my mind."

And here is what I don't get. I would have understood if Maggie had let me go, but Jake? Balls To The Wall, show no mercy, Jake?

"Why are you letting me go?"

"When you go, make sure you leave a letter that sounds convincing. Say you can't take the pressure from dad and Uncle Hightower. Need to start over. Some bullshit like that. Now, get off the phone, I don't want this to get traced back to Maggie."

"Will you tell her I'm sorry again?"

There is silence, then a dial tone.

The cat is rubbing its matted body against my legs. I offer my hand in greeting. He sniffs it, his electric eyes poised on my face. After I pass inspection, he jumps into the car, landing one my lap then moving over to the passenger seat.

Well. Why not?

"You know," I warn him, "I'm a serial killer. Are you sure you want to do this?"

He yawns, then closes his eyes. His purr motor revs and is so loud, I swear I can feel the vibrations.

"I'd call you Justice, but that's fucking predictable, isn't it?" I put the car in drive and back out of the lot. "I'll have to come up with a really good name for you. Something that fits. It'll take awhile, you know, until I can figure out what you're about. But don't worry, we've got a long road trip in front of us."

We've got the rest of our lives.

Detective Bennigan
August 19, Early Morning Hours

The room smells like baby powder and has the oddly comforting odor of sour spit-up. It's bathed in a soft radiance from the star shaped yellow night light.

Sara Kate is sleeping. Her chubby body is wrapped in a pink Onesie. Her cheeks are as plump as her little legs and arms. She reminds me of a tulip before the sun has coaxed it open.

Jake bends over the crib and carefully picks her up. He presses her body against his chest, filling his lungs with her scent.

"Sometimes, I sneak in at night and pick her up and hold her while she's sleeping."

I touch Sara's pudgy foot. It's soft and warm, like the breath of a kitten.

"Sometimes, Maggie, the love I feel for her physically hurts my heart. I thought I could never love anyone or anything as much as I love my wife. This…" he kisses Sara's downy black hair, "is a different love. So pure."

"I know how you feel."

"When I hear about babies dying because someone tossed them in a trash can, or because someone shook them so hard their brains turned to mush…I almost have a fucking panic attack."

I reach out and squeeze his hand. His palm is slick with sweat.

"This baby, my baby…" Jake's eyes glaze with tears. He looks away. "The thought of anyone hurting her…I would go insane with anger and sadness. I don't know how parents can cope with the loss of a child, especially one who has been brutally murdered. How can they go on, Maggie?"

"I don't know Jake. I can't imagine it, but I'm sure every day is a day they have to be pulled through with the help of their family and friends."

Jake lifts Sara's arm and kisses her little fist. She smiles in her sleep.

I sink onto the rocking chair in the corner, focusing outside the window. The emotion in the room, the emotion of the past few hours is drawing me to the rapids and I'm afraid it will pull me completely under.

"Does it get easier as they get older?" He asks.

"I wish I could say yes." On the clothesline in the backyard, white sheets flutter in the breeze. "You just kind of pray to anyone who will listen…you ask that your baby stays safe and protected."

Moonlight spills into the room and swaddles father and daughter in a reverent glow. If there was a camera to capture the moment, the picture would make the cover of Life magazine.

"Jake." I shift my eyes back to the yard. A line of sunflowers borders the picket fence. "You understand that if Nate decides to turn himself in, or he's caught and gives up the dirt on us…you won't be around to hold Sara every night, you won't be able to keep the bed bugs away."

Jake places Sara back in the crib, covering her with a thin blanket embroidered with Peter Rabbit.

"There is more honor in protecting children than there is in protecting pedophiles."

I close my eyes and see the rushing of the waters. I try to swim to the bank of the river. "What about upholding the law? What about the oath you took?"

"I promised to serve and protect. That's exactly what I'm doing. I'd rather spend my life behind bars knowing I tried to make this world a safer place than get a letter of commendation because I was partly responsible for the arrest of someone trying to make this world a better place."

The bank is within my grasp. I reach out and grab twisted roots embedded in the dirt. I open my eyes.

Jake's face is lit with excitement, yet he is serene.

I realize the difference between us is not so much our morals and values, but the confidence we place behind them.

If we were standing on the front line in a battle zone and the General yelled, "Charge!" Jake would be the first person running into the fire. I would hesitate, raise my hand and ask, "What is it we're fighting for again?"

I'm trying to pull my body out of the water, but the river is rising, angry, thrashing against my legs.

"I don't know if I can carry this secret around for the rest of my life."

Jake kneels before me. "In your heart, Maggie…don't you feel what we did was right?"

"The law doesn't give a shit about what I think is right."

He rocks back on his heels and places his hands on mine. He is no longer sweating; his skin is dry, cool. "Forget about this night, Maggie. I know it will be hard at first, but time will erase your worry. Time will chew the edge off your fear. One day, you'll wake up and wonder if this really happened. One day, it will all seem like a dream."

"It's just...I've always wanted to do the honorable thing."

He stands up, retrieves Sara from her slumber once again, and this time, places her in my arms. She squirms, her rosebud mouth quivers. I gently press her against my chest, against my heart. Her eyes open; they are blue as a robin's egg, and they blink at me, once, twice, innocent and trusting. And with a soft sigh, her sweet breath tickling my arm, she gives herself back to dreamland. She lifts her arm, her fist opening, searching in her sleep for something to latch onto. I place my finger in the curve of her palm. Her hand closes, transferring warmth. This nine pound miracle is pulling me out of the rapids. She squeezes and squeezes until my feet are on solid ground, until I'm walking away from the swirling undercurrents. She lets go and her arm falls to the side; I tuck it back under the blanket. She smiles in her sleep and nudges her head closer to my heart.

"I have to get back home to Zoey." I whisper.

2 a.m.

I have just turned off all the lights and am making the climb to my bedroom where I will wait for sleep like a 45-year-old virgin waits for sex, when there is a knock at the door. Badge barks once and his ass bumps my legs as he turns around and runs down the stairs.

I switch the lights back on as I go, hoping it won't be Nate standing behind the door. What if he's come to kill me? Maybe he's that foolish, consumed with fear because we've blown his cover that he's decided to silence the choir.

It's so crazy, a smile stalks my lips as I reach on top of the dining room cabinet and reload my gun.

Crazy, yes, but the idea of Becky being a killer, Luke being a killer, and then discovering Nate is the killer, all have a certain degree of lunacy.

Why would Nate bother knocking? Because all my windows are shut and locked. I don't care how mild the air; I would never leave a window unlatched or open in the middle of night. Ever.

I walk through the living room, dragging my feet, turning a lamp on here, there. Badge is poised at the door, sniffing the air coming through the crack.

Maybe it's Becky. Maybe after she got in her car and turned onto the main road she got to thinking about the carton of orange juice I knocked over as we stood in the kitchen finalizing the new daycare arrangements.

"You're just tired." Becky had laughed, helping me clean up the mess. "This case is stressing you out. It's late; I'm going to head home. Why don't you bring Zoey over tomorrow, we'll relax in the pool and get the details ironed out."

I agreed, gave her a long hug and assured her that I was okay.

I pushed aside the curtain on the front window.

There, under the porch light, stands Luke. Wearing a Flyers baseball cap and a scowl.

I quickly unload the gun and tuck it under the couch cushion.

Fuck. Fuck. Fuck.

I hop around the room, blow air under my armpits that have unleashed a sudden torrent of perspiration.

Badge sits on his haunches and cocks his head to the side. "Have you gone mad?" He questions with his eyes.

Luke knows. Why else would he be standing on my stoop at two in the morning? He must have seen Jake and me staking out Hayden's house. Maybe he watched the whole thing unfold.

Maybe Jake and Nate are sitting in the same jail cell right now.

I open the door. I won't beg mercy. I'll be strong.

"Maggie." He steps inside, briefly offering Badge a pat on the head.

"Hi. It's kinda late isn't it? Did everything go alright?"

The lines around his mouth soften. "Yes, it went okay. I mean, as well, as anything like that can go."

"Good...I guess. I mean..." I shake my head. What *do* I mean?

"You know I stopped by here tonight...Becky told me you were out with Jake." He stuffs his hands in his pockets and trains his eyes on my face. I can't stop the heat from clawing at my cheeks.

"Yeah..." I offer no more.

The only sound in the stillness is that of Badge panting.

I examine the back of my arms, as if I've suddenly noticed they are attached to my body. Flexing to make sure my elbows work.

"I called Jake's house." Luke touches my shoulder.

My arms are no longer interesting.

"I thought of calling your cell but then I thought if you and Jake were in the middle of something..." He rushes into the next sentence, fumbling like a quarterback with greased hands, "Like, if something were bothering you or Jake and you needed to talk to each other and that's why you guys were hanging out." Luke takes a breath, "I didn't mean to imply you guys were doing anything other than talking."

I offer him a weak smile.

"Lucy's mother answered. She told me Jake had gone to work."

I try to swallow, but once again my body starts to shut down. The lump in my throat is the size of a boulder and my saliva gets trapped in my mouth. I feel as if I'm going to choke or suffocate.

"Knowing how aggressive Jake is, how pissed he was that we decided not to surveillance Hayden's house...I kinda figured that might be where you were at."

My lungs trap oxygen...none leaves, none enters. I take breaths as sparingly as possible. I imagine that before they take me to jail, I'll wind up in the hospital on a respirator.

"So, you know, I drive by Hayden's house. See the undercover car, see your little head pop up when I'm almost at the end of the block."

I think I'm going to faint. I reach back, making sure the couch is behind me as I lower myself onto the cushion.

"And I'm driving around the block, ready to come back again and bawl you both out. And then I'm thinking, no, no, I'll call her. So I go to a park down the road and pull into a space and guess what happens?"

I shake my head. Tears sting my eyes and I rest my head in my hands. I wonder if I will possibly receive probation. It could happen. The right judge would show mercy on me because I'm a cop. And to throw a cop into prison is a guaranteed death sentence.

"I see a guy walking his dog." Luke says.

I sit up a bit straighter. The lump in my throat constricts and allows some air through. I cock my head to the side like Badge does when something's loopy.

"That's right." He rocks back on his heels. "There's a young guy, bout my age, walking this ugly mutt that has a head I swear is fucking square. He lets the dog off the leash and it runs up a small embankment to a playground. He circles the swings, rounds the slide, like he's chasing a squirrel. He's running so fast it's comical. I start laughing because this dog looks like his legs won't be able to keep up and he'll topple over and fall end over end down the slope. Then the dog takes off into some trees and the owner cusses and yells and sprints after him."

Badge and I are staring at Luke. It's like he is standing on the middle of a stage and the glare of the spotlight mixed with the bass of his voice is mesmerizing.

"The guy is wearing black sweat pants, black t-shirt, the dog's leash is sailing behind him as he runs. And then it hits me…" Luke bounces the heel of his hand off his forehead, knocking his baseball cap to the floor. Badge snatches it and runs out of the living room, his tail wagging in joy, sending waves of cool air to fan me.

"You think I'm the Pedophile Predator, Maggie. You and Jake were staking out the house thinking I might strike. You probably thought the whole abortion thing was a set up. You probably thought I was against surveillancing the house because I wanted to kill Hayden."

I start to shake my head no. No No No. And then I stop. Because, really, I *had* been suspicious of him.

"I remember when you found the articles I saved about the Pedophile Predator. You had this look on your face; I couldn't name it at the time, but now I realize it was disbelief. And the night you found my clothes and the leash in the shed…you withdrew from me, became distant. But I was too caught up in what was going on with my old girlfriend to pay much attention. But tonight, it made sense. I got it."

I stare at his shoes. I have the urge to smile out of sheer relief that I'm not going to jail. But there could be more to the story.

"Am I right?"

I nod. I stare at the chipped pink polish on my toenails. "Luke, I didn't intend to set you up. Jake called me and told me were going somewhere. I never told him of my suspicions."

"But you never told me either, Maggie."

Tears sneak out the corners of my eyes. They fall onto my hands, the salt stinging my skin where the puncture from the splinter had not yet healed.

"I sort of understand why you wouldn't confront me with your suspicions. You had a hard time dealing with my past, knowing I'd been a sort of playboy." He rolls his eyes, his voice melts like butter left on a warm stove. "That's enough to contend with, but then…" he shakes his head, "You thought I could be a…serial killer" He laughs. He laughs and laughs and laughs so hard he falls against the door. Badge rushes in at the sounds coming from the living room, the Flyers hat still clamped under his teeth, stringy drool dripping from his mouth.

I find myself laughing. Not because it's funny ha ha, but because Luke's laughter rolls over and in me. Tears stream out of our eyes, our bellies convulse, and our bodies shake. It is the sound of mirth, but really, I know, it disguises our sadness. His pain at the thought someone could imagine he was a killer. My pain for the last few weeks. If I didn't laugh, I would collapse into a hysterical weeping heap at his feet and confess everything.

"I think you're the best fucking thing in the world, Maggie Bennigan. I really do." He finally wipes his eyes with the sleeve of his shirt. He takes the ball cap from Badge and lowers himself beside me. "You really knocked me on my ass that first night we got together, and every night after that. I thought you could be the one. But the most important thing to me is trust."

I have nothing to say. My body slowly quiets until a stillness settles and I can feel it all the way to my soul.

"I thought, you know, the whole playboy issue would work itself out quickly as long as I treated you like you were the best thing to happen since the Flyers won the Stanley Cup in 1975. That's reasonable, right?"

I nod. Bracing myself.

"But...Maggie, to think I'm capable of being a serial killer..."

"I was trying to figure it all out, Luke. This case has made me crazy." I try to reason. "I thought if you were the killer I'd...well, I'd..."

He waits.

I don't know how to explain things to him when I'm not sure what my intentions had been. "I was falling in love with you, you know. I was trying to decide if I was going to somehow help you out. I was trying to decide which was more important, my job, or you?" And now, as the words fall out of my mouth, they don't sound right. They spill on the floor and spread like oil, not sinking into the wood, only smothering it.

His eyes search mine. For a moment, I forget about Nate. For a moment, it seems like the worst that happened tonight is what's happening at this moment.

"I can't decide if that's a good thing or a bad thing." Luke says.

"Well, imagine how I felt."

He smiles. Like I'm the new girl at school standing in the lunchroom, searching for a place to fit in. He's the kid who would offer to make room for me because he feels sorry for me.

"It could have been so right, this thing between us. But, for whatever reason, it's just not the right time. I wish trust wasn't such an important issue with me, but it's the one thing I value above all else. And if I compromise on the thing I prize most..."

I had thought the man sitting beside me was a chipped diamond. Turns out he's a priceless gem.

"I am so sorry." My voice is barely audible.

"Me too. I wish I wasn't so…anal." He squeezes my hand. "I'm not saying I'm perfect Maggie. I've made my share of mistakes, you know? I'm just saying there are some things that I can't compromise on."

"Like you're girlfriend thinking you're a serial killer." I stand up and walk him to the door.

"It's gonna drive me crazy working the case with you." He gently brushes away a strand of hair that has fallen across my face.

"Me too."

"I know it's so…passé, but, can we be friends?" He opens the door and pauses before crossing the threshold.

"Of course." I lie. I know I will start to distance myself from him because of what I know, because I don't want to hurt him any more than I already have.

He kisses me on the forehead.

"Luke." I grab hold of his wrists. It's now or never. If I tell him everything, there could be some salvation. I could cut a deal with the District Attorney's office.

"Yes?"

From upstairs, Zoey's voice cries out, "Mommmmy!"

"I really am sorry…for everything."

I close the door; shutting out Luke and Nate and Jake.

Everything that was will be swallowed by the night and everything that will be shall rise with the dawning of the sun.

September 7, Saturday.

The water laps at the yellow raft I'm stretched out on. My hands are submersed in the water, my wrists make little swirls, creating circles that captivate me.

Becky floats next to me; her blue raft bumps mine gently.

Zoey is napping and I'm on my third day of vacation.

"Over three weeks since the Pedophile Predator's hit." Becky says.

"Yep." My eyes cannot break free from the rings of water that are growing wider as my hands spin faster. "Thanks for keeping the pool open one more day for me."

"As long as we keep having 80 degree weather…I don't care if we don't close the pool until December."

Luke is back at the FBI office.

Nate's sudden disappearance didn't raise as much of a ruckus as I had braced myself for. Rumor was he was just a young man trying to find himself; trying to break the mold that was imposed on him by his father and uncle.

I've finally started to sleep a few hours a night. Jake was right, time softens.

"I'm so glad they found David Westerfield guilty." Becky grabs onto the side of the pool. She straddles her raft, sitting up; she reaches for her Diet Coke.

"Me too." I pull my hands out of the water and tuck them under my head.

"He better get the death penalty." She picks up the newspaper.

I gingerly turn over on my back, water rushes in the gaps I've created by moving. My skin prickles with goose bumps.

"If he molested and killed Susan or Zoey and they found him not guilty and I knew he was guilty? I'd kill him myself." She pushes off the side and her raft bumps mine again, sending me sailing to the middle of the pool.

"What if you got caught Beck?"

"I'd just make sure my best friend investigated the case."

I lift my head to look at her.

"What does that mean?"

"You once thought I was a killer, remember? And you didn't turn me in."

"Well, deep down inside, I didn't really think you were the killer."

We float in silence for a few minutes. The sun tries to lull me to sleep but I fight it.

"Well, this is interesting." She holds the paper out, squinting behind her sunglasses.

"In Austin Texas, there is a serial killer on the loose."

"There's a serial killer on the loose in practically every state." The warm rays hug my shoulders; caress my back.

"The victims are five men and they all have one connection. They all have prior convictions."

I prop myself up on my elbows. She lowers her head and gazes at me over the top of her Ray Ban's.

"The murdered men were convicted sexual predators, their victims were children."

I slip off my raft and dive under the water, the quick bite of coolness sinking into my skin. It takes my limbs three strokes until I'm almost under her raft. As my body surfaces, the motion knocks Becky off her raft, sending her into the water. The newspaper falls into the pool, the thinly inked paper sucks up the water.

"Jesus, Maggie." Becky laughs, shaking her wet head and grabbing onto her raft with her arms, her legs floating behind her.

The paper tears in my hands as I try to rescue it. I scoop it up and place it in a wet, mushy ball on the concrete.

"Sorry about your paper." I hang on to the side of the pool, water dripping from my chin, making a small puddle on the concrete.

"No big deal. I only subscribe to it for the Sunday coupons anyway."

The backdoor opens and Zoey stares at us, blinking in the afternoon glare.

I pull myself out and wrap a towel around my waist. "Hey baby." I hold out my arms.

"What do you think about that?" Becky calls out.

Zoey wipes her eyes. "Can I go swimming now?"

"Sure honey."

Her bathing suit is under her clothes and I help her shimmy out of her shirt and shorts.

"Maggie? What are you thinking?"

"I'm thinking I don't live in Austin, Texas. It's not my jurisdiction." I walk down the steps into the shallow end. Zoey stands at the edge of the pool. Her lopsided grin is small, bright, and innocent.

"Mommy, will you catch me?"

I hold out my arms, trusting myself, trusting the universe.

"Jump Sweetheart, jump."

0-595-28812-X